ESCAPE INTO
DAYLIGHT

Escape Into Daylight

P - 6 8

Geoffrey Household

An Atlantic Monthly Press Book

Little, Brown and Company
Boston **Toronto**

Second Printing

Library of Congress Cataloging in Publication Data

Household, Geoffrey, 1900–
    Escape into daylight.

    "An Atlantic Monthly Press book."
    SUMMARY: In danger of losing their lives, two
kidnapped youngsters being held in a ruined abbey make
several desperate attempts to escape.
    [1.   Kidnapping—Fiction]   I.   Title.
PZ7.H8158Es3   [Fic]   76–10162
ISBN 0-316-37436-9

ATLANTIC–LITTLE, BROWN BOOKS
ARE PUBLISHED BY
LITTLE, BROWN AND COMPANY
IN ASSOCIATION WITH
THE ATLANTIC MONTHLY PRESS

CONTENTS

*This Book
is for Richard and Luke*

I

Kidnapped

It was dark as before the beginning of the world. Blackness. Nothing. At first the boy thought he must be at home, but when his eyes had been open a second longer he knew that he could not be; not even on a clouded, moonless night was there such darkness in his room. The last thing he remembered was being thrown on the floor of the van, held down and half smothered by a rug.

He must have lost consciousness in the van and now had arrived somewhere and was awake. At least he supposed so, but the silence and the darkness were unlike anything he had ever experienced when awake. His heart began to beat very fast as two imaginary terrors hit him. The first was that he had been buried alive. That fear was at once proved to be ridiculous. He wriggled his arms free of whatever was keeping them close to his sides, flung them wide and found plenty of space all around him. The second fear was that he had gone blind. That was not so ridiculous.

The boy felt and rubbed his eyes. Nothing seemed wrong with them. Since he could neither see nor hear, he tried what touch and smell could tell him. He discovered that he was in a sleeping bag. Beneath it were one or two folded blankets. Beyond the bag was a hard floor feeling as if it were paved with stone. Smell was of damp. That and the stones brought up a memory of the day when his parents had taken him to visit a ruined castle. He had asked if there were any dungeons, and the custodian had unlocked an iron gate, as a special favour, and led them down steps to see a dungeon which had once been below the level of the moat. It had smelt just like the place where he was.

The boy felt that he ought to have the courage to jump up and explore, but got no further than wriggling out of the bag and sitting on it. The sleeping bag, after all, was the only object he could be certain about; away from it everything was unknown and he might never be able to find his way back. Somebody must have put him there and the same somebody would expect to find him there. He considered yelling at the top of his voice and badly wanted to. He had to remind himself that he was a farmer's son and well used to darkness – though not such darkness as this.

When his heart had stopped beating so fast, it seemed to him that the silence was not so complete as he thought. He heard a very faint, regular whispering which might be far away or very close. It was only when the sound stopped and was succeeded by a sob that he realised he had been listening to the breathing of another person.

'Is anyone there?' he asked.

'Oh! Oh, yes!'

'Where am I?'

'I don't know. You're where I am. I saw you being brought down.'

The boy nerved himself to ask the question which terrified him more than anything else.

'Am I blind?'

'No, of course you're not. In daytime there's a tiny bit of light once your eyes get used to it.'

'Where are you?'

It was impossible to tell where the girl's voice was coming from. It sounded as if it were everywhere at once.

'Not far. But there are pillars and things. If you feel your way round the wall you'll come to me.'

'But where's the wall?'

'You're lying quite close to it. It's on your right.'

The boy cautiously moved away from the sleeping bag.

'There isn't any wall,' he said.

'Well, perhaps it's on your left.'

Girls, he thought, often said right when they meant left though they knew very well which was which. But of course she could not be sure. There wasn't any right or left unless she knew which end of him his head was. And it might be difficult to spot that when somebody had carried him into the dark and dropped him down.

He returned to the bag, found the wall and followed it round very slowly until he was on top of the voice.

'What are you doing here?' he asked.

'I've been kidnapped. And you too, I expect. Who's your father? Is he very rich?'

'No. He farms near Hanborough. He's doing all right, but we're not at all rich.'

'That's funny. I live near Hanborough too. You didn't see them grab me, did you?'

No, he had seen nothing wrong and done nothing

wrong, he told her. That morning, which was Saturday, he had taken a bus into town to get some advice from his favourite shop. A fine shop, he said. It sold shot-guns and cartridges and decoy wood pigeons and fishing tackle. What he wanted to know was how to make an eel trap and whether he should use netting or basketwork – all because his father had said it was silly to pay good money for eels when anyone could catch them if he knew how. His friend at the shop said he believed the best traps were of basketwork and he would try to get him one cheap. Then, dreaming of all the eels he would catch in the river or the canal, he went off to look at the wall.

The wall amused him. It was better than a comic. The older gang at school wrote all sorts of messages on it – some to each other, some to girls, some about football. Most could just as well have been whispered or shouted, but it was more fun to chalk them on the wall when no one was looking. The boy could not make sense of half the secrets which were there and that was why they fascinated him, just like the bits of a newspaper which were vague. The smooth bricks recorded goings-on in a life which would be part of his own in another year or two but which he could not yet share.

The wall went round part of the gasworks on a street which led out into the country. A fair amount of traffic passed, but few people on foot since there were no shops. On the other side of the street was waste ground where a derelict factory was being pulled down to make room for a housing estate. The boy always felt a little guilty at following the wall and stopping to read what was there, so he used to approach it across the waste ground and wait till the coast was clear.

The street was not on his way to and from school, and he seldom saw any of the older boys actually writing. He was sure that none of them would be there on a Saturday morning and was surprised to see that somebody was – but a man, not a boy or girl. First he read all the doodles and inscriptions and then he went back to the beginning and started to scribble on the bricks himself. The man had his back to him, so the boy slipped unseen behind a pile of broken concrete by the roadside and watched him. He wore blue overalls and a hat pushed well down over his eyes. Whenever he saw anyone coming, he pulled out a steel tape measure and a spirit level as if he were a builder on the job of cleaning or repairing the wall, but when the street was empty he returned to writing something in red chalk, moving along and picking his spaces. At that distance the boy could only see that he seemed to be scribbling numbers.

It did not take long. When the man had finished he looked up and down the street. Seeing nobody on foot and no car, he started to walk quickly out of town.

'I recognised him,' the boy announced excitedly. 'He was Rupert Falconer, my very favourite film star. And I've seen him dozens of times on the telly. He was the private eye in . . .'

'He's my father,' the girl said. 'I'm Carrie Falconer.'

'Your father! But why doesn't he rescue you?'

'I think he has to pay to get me back.'

'He ought to come charging in here with a gun.'

'He isn't like that in real life, you know. Mary and

he had a row once because he wouldn't set a trap to catch a mouse.'

'Well, I like mice too.'

'But Mary doesn't. What was he writing on the wall?'

'Numbers. I'll tell you what happened. I wanted his autograph, so I ran after him and caught him up just as he was getting into his car which was parked round the next corner. He looked a bit annoyed but he gave me his autograph. And then I asked him if the camera was somewhere in the factory while he was writing on the wall. I thought I might be in the picture, you see, though I hadn't noticed anybody filming him. He said there wasn't any camera and he wasn't really writing. He was just trying to see what sort of a shot it would make. Then he drove off fast. So I went back to the wall and looked at what he had been writing. It was a whole lot of numbers as I thought. He had really been writing, not pretending. I took them down because I thought they might be shown on the screen and then I could open my notebook and tell everyone what I'd seen.'

'What car did he use?' she asked.

'A green Mercedes.'

'Well, that's ours.'

'And the other car was a grey van.'

'What other car?'

'It came along while I was making a note of the numbers and passed me and came back again and stopped. The driver asked me what I was doing. I said I was taking down numbers which Rupert Falconer had written on the wall. He thought for a bit and whispered to another man in the car, and then he said: "I'm the director of the film he's in. Would you like to see his house?" He was rather fat and very respectable looking, like an auctioneer or something.'

'Like a butler,' she said. 'That's the man who called for me.'

'I've never seen a butler, but he might be. Well, I hadn't much time to catch my bus and Mr Falconer wasn't very pleased to be spoken to, so I said I thought it had better be another day. But the director chap said there was no time like the present and after we had called on Mr Falconer he would run me back home if I liked. So I told him where I lived and got in the back of the van, and the other man got in the back too. I didn't care for him. He was always smiling. I remember the driver saying: "Now! It's all clear!" And then the other man threw me on the floor and put his hand over my mouth and I think he pricked me with something.'

'Just like they did to me,' she said. 'What's your name?'

'Mike. Michael Prowse. How did they get you?'

'It was because Rupert and Mary aren't living together. They had another row.'

'That's your father and mother?'

'Yes. They like me to call them Rupert and Mary, but I think it's silly. Well, Mary always fetches me from school. But yesterday she was late. While I was waiting for her a car drove up and the driver said that he was a chauffeur from the studio and that Rupert and Mary were at the flat he keeps in London and wanted me to be there. I was so happy that they had made it up that I got in the car at once and sat down on something

13

sharp. The chauffeur said he was very sorry and that his wife must have left a needle on the seat. And the next thing I knew I was lying here.'

'Alone in the dark?'

'Yes. But somebody was listening and when I started to scream he came down and told me that if I stayed quiet I wouldn't be hurt, and in a few days I could go home.'

'You've been screaming some more, Carrie. I know because your voice is so hoarse.'

'I couldn't help it. But nobody told me to shut up, so I'm sure we can't be heard outside at all.'

'Where do you think we are?'

'I don't know. When there's a little light to see by, it looks a bit like a church.'

Mike sat down by her side and the two began to talk about themselves and their lives. They found that they were both twelve. Carrie had always lived and gone to school in London till her parents bought a country house near Hanborough, and now she was at a posh day school nearby and didn't think much of it.

'What's it like, being the daughter of a film star?'

'All right. But it doesn't do Rupert any good to be famous.'

Suddenly she began to cry. She sobbed that it was because she was so thankful to have someone to cry to.

'Didn't you cry when you were alone?'

'Not much. I screamed but I didn't have a good cry.'

Mike heard movement somewhere above them. Carrie told him that it would probably be the man with food. Then there was a pool of light from an electric lantern which revealed stone steps and a pair of legs coming down them. Their visitor had a nylon stocking over his head with two holes for his eyes. Mike recognised the voice of the man with the fixed smile who had smothered and drugged him.

'Supper!' he said, putting down two cans of cocoa and a pot of thick soup with bread and two spoons in it. 'And here's your breakfast in this bag! You'd better make it last because it's all you are going to get till tomorrow night.'

'How long are you going to keep us here?'

'As long as we have to, son. And that depends on our Mr Falconer.'

'He'll pay,' Carrie said. 'But it isn't fair to keep Michael Prowse. What do you want him for?'

'He's the last dam' thing we want. He'd have been all right if he hadn't recognised your father.'

'Can you let my parents know you've got me?' Mike asked.

'Is it likely? What you'd better hope is that the police never have a clue to where you are – because if they find out it's going to be very hard for us to know what to do with you. Now get on with your grub while you've a light to eat by!'

Mike could see his partner for the first time. She was dressed in school uniform, and had long, fair hair, tied with a ribbon at the back, and big, clever eyes. She seemed a bit on the fat side but had long legs. Carrie ought to be able to run, he thought, if we ever have a chance.

The cocoa was cold but the soup was not bad. Mike had little appetite after being drugged, so he let

Carrie eat most of it while he examined his surroundings as far as the lantern could show them. The place seemed to be a cellar but was large enough for a village church. Short, massive pillars with arches over them held up the roof, marching along in a shadowy line until they disappeared into blackness. Above the steps was a round hole through which the man had come. Nothing at all was on the stone flags of the floor except the two sleeping bags and a small drum of drinking water.

'If we have to stay here, you might make us a bit more comfortable,' Carrie said.

'What do you want?'

'Can we have some light?'

'And more blankets,' Mike added, for he was getting colder and colder.

'Get in your bag if you're not warm enough! You can chatter to each other just as well. About light – well, I'll see what the others say and if we have any candles.'

He gathered up the pot, the two cans and the lantern and went back up the steps. He put back a cover over the hole and they heard him slide home a bolt.

Mike went shivering back to his bed and was nearly asleep when the man returned.

'Here's a couple of candles and some matches!' he said. 'Don't set yourselves on fire! And just remember the light can't be seen and you can't be heard. So it's no good trying any monkey tricks.'

When he had gone and shut them up again, they lit the candles and explored their prison. Stones, damp, arches and darkness – that was all. Beyond the great cellar where they were they found another one, rather smaller and with the pillars closer together. Here and there smooth, brown roots had forced their way through the roof like snakes. Coming from one crack was a shoot with shrivelled buds on it which were white instead of green. Air could get in but there was no way out except the steps.

In this second cellar there was a semicircle of old brickwork standing out from the stone wall and running right up to the vaulted roof. Everywhere else the walls and angles were regular as the inside of a box. The curved bow of smooth brick offered no hope at all. It looked as if it had been built as a buttress to support the roof.

The two prisoners returned to their sleeping bags and put out the candles. Carrie, exhausted by two days of fear and loneliness, slept deeply. Mike remained awake much longer. He came to the conclusion that the police were bound to trace the kidnappers through their cars, but if they escaped or refused to talk when arrested he and Carrie might never be found. Then what would happen if there was no food and no light? He only hoped that Rupert Falconer was making so much money that he could pay whatever had been demanded.

When he awoke the great cellar was not quite so black. The entrance at the top of the steps was covered by an iron grating through which came thin strips of twilight. He got up and felt his way into the second chamber, which had been bothering his dreams. Once through the archway there was no light at all, and he could not define what it was that he expected to find.

He was hungry, so he felt his way back to Carrie and gently woke her up.

The bag left for their breakfast held ham sandwiches, a packet of oatmeal biscuits and a pot of jam. They ate the sandwiches and left the biscuits for later as the masked man had advised.

'He never comes down during the day,' Carrie said.

'Is it always the same screw?'

'What's a screw?'

'It's what chaps in the nick call the prison officer. If he only turns up at night, it means that he might be seen coming here. So there must be people somewhere above us.'

'Unless we are right out in wild country.'

'Well, there's always somebody about on the land – farmers or gamekeepers or hikers,' Mike said. 'How long were you in the car?'

'I don't know.'

'Nor do I. That's the worst of it. We might be any-where. It might have taken them only an hour to drive us here, or all day and half the night.'

2

Wasted Ransom

Rupert Falconer opened the morning paper and exclaimed:

'Oh my God! What are we to do?'

Mary looked over his shoulder. Carrie would have been happy to know that she was at home again.

'It's the boy who saw me writing up the number of the bank account. The devils have got him too!'

'Then we have to go to the police whether we like it or not,' she said firmly.

'We can't! We mustn't! They might kill them both. They have nothing to lose.'

'They need not know we have called in the police, Rupert. We have no right not to tell these poor parents what must have happened to their son.'

The disappearance of Michael Prowse was on the front page. He was last seen at about half past eleven on Saturday morning when he visited the sporting goods shop of Messrs Edwards in Hanborough to ask about eel traps. Mr Edwards, who knew him well, said that he seemed full of beans and was a very intelligent young chap whom he was always pleased to see. Nobody knew where Michael had gone after that, but a boy answering his description had been seen crossing the waste ground by the gasworks. The derelict factory nearby had been thoroughly searched. As he was known to be interested in water, frogmen were down inspecting the river and canal, but the boy was an excellent swimmer and would have come to no harm if he fell in. Police, the paper said, suspected foul play.

'Show me the kidnappers' note again!' Mary Falconer asked her husband.

He took the square of paper from his wallet, unfolded it and laid it on the breakfast table. The message was composed of words cut from a newspaper and pasted on the sheet so as to avoid clues which might be discovered from handwriting or a typewriter.

'We have your daughter in a safe place from which she cannot escape. It will cost you £100,000 to get her back. If you tell the police or the newspapers we may be forced to go away and leave her. She cannot ever be found and will die of starvation.

'You earned £100,000 from your last film and you put the money in a secret, numbered account at the Munster Creditanstalt in Zurich. We have a similar, secret account at the same branch.

'You will authorise the bank to transfer the money to our account as soon as we give them the number of yours. We have arranged that no other instructions will be required. Thus it is unnecessary for you to know the number of our account, but we must know the number of yours.

'We require that number immediately. At the south side of Hanborough gasworks you will find a brick wall on which children write and draw. There you will write the number in red chalk so that the first figure is below the white painted heart and the last above UP THE HAMMERS. When the money has been transferred your daughter will be released.'

'She'll be back the day after tomorrow,' Rupert Falconer asserted, trying to sound as if he were sure of it.
'But what about the boy?'
'Why should they do him any harm?'
'He might know their names, faces, anything.'
'It's not likely.'
'It's very likely, Rupert. We have to tell the police and trust them to see that nothing about Carrie leaks out.'
'We daren't go into a police station in case we are watched. And we must not have policemen calling here.'
'I shall ring them up and leave it to them,' Mary said firmly.

She dialled Hanborough police and asked for the officer in charge of the Prowse case. She had difficulty in getting through to him, for she would not give her name or her reason. But it was always hard to stop Mary Falconer when her mind was made up, and eventually she had the Chief Superintendent on the line.

'I can explain the disappearance of Michael Prowse,' she told him. 'But I dare not come to the police station or ask you to my house. It might be dangerous for him. What do you suggest?'

'Walk past the *White Horse* at eleven o'clock, madam. That is a small pub in Castle Street behind the Cornmarket. One of my sergeants will be there in plain clothes. He will be able to judge the importance of your information and will report to me. How will he recognise you?'

'I shall be with my husband. And my husband's face will be familiar to your sergeant even if he can't quite remember who he is.'

'Of course he will know who I am,' Rupert said.

'Will he? What about the time when that woman thought you were the Member of Parliament?'

'We are very much alike.'

'You are not in the least alike, Rupert. Come on! We have no time to lose.'

They parked the car in Hanborough and walked through side streets to the *White Horse*. Nobody was there except a shabby individual obviously impatient for a drink and waiting for the pub to open. They never realised that he was the sergeant they had come to meet until he slid off into the yard at the back of the pub and beckoned to them.

He did recognise the actor – much to Rupert's satisfaction – and assured him at once that the police would be very careful.

'I realise that anything you do, Mr Falconer, is of interest to the public.'

Even so they told him as little as possible: simply that it was indeed Michael Prowse who had been crossing the waste ground and that the reason for his kidnapping was that he had been making notes of numbers scribbled on the gasworks wall. How they discovered it and a great deal more they were prepared to explain to the Chief Superintendent and no one else.

'Know Backley Wood?' the sergeant asked.

'Very well.'

'Be at the footbridge over the railway at midday. I think I can say the Chief will be there. Are you likely to be followed?'

'We don't know.'

'Well, we will see that you are not.'

The Falconers drove out to Backley Wood, more miserable than ever because Carrie loved to picnic there in the pale green light under the beeches. A deserted lane crossed the railway by a narrow bridge, which must have been built a hundred years earlier to give some farmer access to his fields on the other side of the line and was now so little used that grass had grown over the surface.

A car was waiting on the far side of the bridge. Beyond it, under the trees, they could see another – near enough to take action if necessary, far enough away to ensure privacy for the Falconers and the Chief Superintendent.

He left his car and joined them. He was a lean, little man with a deeply-tanned face – not very impressive in build but with the eyes and mouth of an experienced commander. Mary Falconer at once felt sure of his discretion, and that she wouldn't like to be one of his policemen who talked out of turn.

They showed him the ransom note and told him how Michael Prowse had watched the writing on the wall and recognised his favourite actor.

'I see. Well, that will save us wasting a lot of time. And you have told no one that your daughter is missing?'

'No one. We want to pay and get it over.'

'You followed their instructions, Mr Falconer?'

'Yes, at once.'

'As we have proof that a criminal offence has been committed we can compel the Swiss bank to reveal who are the owners of the account to which your money was transferred.'

Mary challenged him fiercely.

'I won't have it, Superintendent!' she cried. 'We love her! Don't you understand that we love her? It's all very well for you to stand there like a lump of wood in uniform, but she is our daughter. If you start your damned official enquiries at the bank she might never be released!'

'Calm yourself, Mrs Falconer! We need not do it yet. I agree that your daughter is in real danger. We will not let it be known that she has disappeared. All our enquiries will be concerned with the kidnapping of the boy, which comes to the same thing. What have you told her school?'

'That she's at home ill.'

'Somebody must have noticed the car which picked her up.'

'Nobody did,' Mary said. 'When I got to the school very late and was told she had left, I thought it must be my husband or one of the studio chauffeurs who had picked her up. Oh, why haven't people got any eyes! Only two girls had seen the car at all. They just said it was black and of course they didn't notice the number.'

'Certainly false anyway,' the Chief Superintendent remarked. 'Why were you late?'

'The garage said that somebody had put water in the petrol tank.'

'The gang had it well worked out. Must have been

24

watching your movements for days! Now, Mr Falconer, I imagine you receive a lot of fan mail and that you have a secretary to deal with it. How did the kidnappers ensure that you and only you would open this letter?'

'I found it on the windshield of my car behind the wiper. My car was in the studio car park and the envelope just had "Rupert" written on it. So I thought it was a note from a friend who hadn't been able to find me and I opened it then and there.'

'A lot of people in the car park?'

'Plenty. I reckoned that somebody must have been watching to make sure that I got the note and read it, but it was hopeless to try to guess who it was.'

'Yes. Well, no doubt I shall have more questions for you later. Meanwhile Mr and Mrs Prowse must be told the truth. You realise that?'

'It's the only reason why we came to you,' Mary said.

'But will they keep their mouths shut?' Falconer asked anxiously. 'What sort of people are they?'

'Mr Jack Prowse farms three hundred acres of good land and is well liked and respected. Mrs Prowse is a warm and responsible woman who gives a lot of her time to local activities. Jack and Janet of the Manor Farm – that's what they are known as for miles around.'

'But everything I do is news and worth money,' the actor complained. 'And they are just plain farmers.'

'They have kept more secrets than yours in their time, Mr Falconer. I shall want to bring you both together with them this afternoon.'

'What they call confrontation? To see if the stories fit?'

'They do fit, and there is no question of confrontation. I should like to hear you talk about your children and what they are likely to do. Keep their heads? Break down? Work out how to escape? Try to arouse pity?'

'Carrie would play that one,' Mary Falconer said.

'There you are, you see! All this may help us. We have no line at all on the gang, so the next best thing is to learn about the children. A description of Carrie, please!'

'A very lovely young thing,' said her father. 'Fair-haired, blue-eyed and graceful.'

'She is not lovely at all yet,' Mary snapped. 'Puppy fat, Superintendent, but tall for her age.'

'Quite so, Mrs Falconer. Fathers are inclined to exaggerate. Now, the meeting with the Prowses will not take place at Hanborough in case you are seen together. I will arrange it at Northam this afternoon where none of you will be expected. But we will take no chances. So I suggest you travel by public transport and walk to the police station. Go in the back way and ask for me! Mr and Mrs Prowse will be with me.'

The Falconers drove back to Hanborough and went to Northam by an afternoon train. They found that they would have a longish walk to the police station and took a taxi. The Chief Superintendent had advised them to walk, but they were desperately impatient for news. They got out when they were not far from the police station, but as they were approaching the back entrance the taxi passed them and the driver gave a cheerful wave.

'He recognised me,' Rupert said. 'But it doesn't matter. He can't know where we are going.'

26

'I don't think there is anywhere else on this street where we could be going,' Mary answered uneasily.

They passed through a yard where police cars were parked and then up a few steps to the back door of the station. They were led straight to an office where the Superintendent was sitting with Mike's parents. Jack Prowse was a big, red-faced man over six feet high and broad in proportion, yet no one who talked to him could feel small in his presence for he always had a friendly, interested smile. His wife was a pretty woman, dark and plump. She would have had a merry face, Mary thought, in normal life but now looked drawn with anxiety and lack of sleep.

The parents found little to say to each other beyond exclamations of sympathy, seated as they were in a line before the Superintendent. He opened up his questions at once, asking if Michael Prowse often visited the wall.

'I don't know,' his father replied. 'He had his secrets like any other boy. And then one day – when he felt like it – out they would come.'

'Independent sort of character?'

'That he was! And that was what we wanted.'

'His teachers tell me he had a lot of imagination.'

Janet Prowse agreed but said he used it on things, not people.

'Carrie is just the opposite. She's clever with people,' Mary said, 'and all for a quiet life if she can get them to do what she wants.'

'What I am wondering is whether much violence had to be used to get them,' the Superintendent explained.

Mr Prowse said he thought Mike would fall for a good story. Mary Falconer believed that Carrie would not. She added with a shade of embarrassment, 'But if the kidnapper said he was a chauffeur from the studio, and if she had reason to think that we were both together in London, she might have been – well, too eager to be on her guard.'

'I see. The kidnappers must have held her down and put her to sleep as soon as they were clear of the school. But they could have risked taking Mike a bit further before fixing him. With luck we may find someone who saw the boy with them in the car. Have you any comment on the photographs which have been circulated, Mr Prowse?'

'Near enough. Dark, wide mouth, brown-eyed. They say he looks like me, but he won't grow so tall.'

'What's worrying me,' his mother said, 'is that Mike was only wearing a sweater and jeans.'

'Well, it's July and hot at that, Mrs Prowse. And you both say he's as tough as nails.'

'You've had no demand for ransom?' Falconer asked Jack Prowse.

'No. I wish to hell there had been. I'd have sold everything I have to get Mike back.'

'They'll release him with Carrie,' Mary said. 'They must! Surely they must?'

Nobody made any remark. It was so obvious that the kidnappers had nothing to gain by letting Mike go.

The Falconers signed their statements, said goodbye to Mr and Mrs Prowse and went out as they had come in – down a passage and out at the back of the station. Then Janet raced after them as if they had forgotten something in the office, and at the door threw her arms round Mary and murmured how sorry she was for her and how in the cold police office she could not express it. Standing at the top of the steps, both burst into tears and hugged each other. There was a flash and a click. A photographer who had crouched in the angle between steps and wall gave a casual nod and bolted out of the yard into the street before anyone could stop him.

At once they returned to the Superintendent and told him what had happened.

'The only hope is that he was after a shot of Mrs Prowse,' Rupert Falconer said, 'and didn't recognise Mary or me.'

'He could not know that the Prowses were here. Somebody knew that you were.'

'That taxi driver! He must have been shooting off his big mouth on the rank or in a pub or somewhere that I had come into the police station. And some blasted newshawk heard him and thought there might be a story in it.'

'I'll try to get hold of him,' the Superintendent said. 'But there's a big case on at the Assizes and a dozen reporters from the national papers whom we don't know. Did you notice the number of the taxi?'

'No. Who does?'

Later in the afternoon the police traced the taxi driver. Yes, he had recognised Rupert Falconer. Yes, he had told his pals in their usual café and they had all wondered why the police wanted to talk to the actor. Yes, there had been two strangers who joined in the conversation and quickly left.

Nothing could be done. And when next day the Falconers ran through all the morning papers they found the picture. It was clear and good. The caption under it was outwardly quite harmless:

JANET PROWSE COMFORTED BY MARY FALCONER

So if and when the kidnappers saw it they would know that Rupert Falconer had appealed to the police after all and that they risked being traced and arrested if they ever collected their hundred thousand pounds.

All that day the Falconers waited for news, praying that the gang had already drawn out the ransom from the bank, covered their tracks and disappeared. Rupert stayed by the telephone hoping that every call would be from police or a stranger to tell him that a girl had been found who said she was Carrie Falconer. Mary waited at the gate and watched every passing car in case it should stop for an instant and push her daughter out on to the pavement. But by nightfall nothing whatever had happened to tell them that they would ever see her again.

3

The Well

When the children had finished their breakfast on the third day of their imprisonment, Mike remarked:

'I wonder what is behind that brickwork. It's been bothering me all night – in between dreams, you know. Suppose there was an old staircase?'

'We can never find out anyway.'

'We might. That mortar is all damp and rotten. I think I could pick it out with my knife. Do they go into that second cellar much?'

'They never have yet. It's not very nice in there.'

'Well, we can't help that. Let's imagine there's a notice of GENTLEMEN in the right corner and LADIES in the left.'

'Powder Room,' said Carrie, which made them both laugh.

They wrapped blankets round them for warmth and went through into the smaller vault, taking a lit candle with them which they put out when Mike's fingers had got used to the work. It was a pleasant occupation picking away at the mortar, and it did not take him long to slip out a brick. He worked away until Carrie had stacked a pile of a dozen bricks and then said he couldn't go on any longer.

'Fingers sore?' she asked.

'No, they are all right. But I'm shivering too

much. The blanket won't stay on while I work.'

'I had a poncho when it was in fashion. That kept me beautifully warm,' Carrie said.

'What's a poncho?'

'Just like a blanket with a hole cut in the middle for your head.'

'That's an idea! I'll go back to bed and see if I can cut a hole in two blankets. It shouldn't be difficult if you hold them tight.'

He snuggled down in bed while Carrie bent over him stretching the blankets. In fact cutting the hole with a blunt knife was a lot more difficult than picking out mortar, but at last it was done and they put on their ponchos. They could not run about to get warm for fear of crashing into pillars, so they danced opposite one another by the light of a candle with Carrie humming all the pop songs she knew.

Mike was now ready for more work on the puzzling, bow-shaped column, and by the time that greyness had faded away from the cracks in the roof and the grating he had removed some thirty bricks from the face.

When the whole cellar was pitch black the usual man, whom they now called Screw, came down with their supper – a pot of thick stew, buttered bread and cheese, and the bag of sandwiches for next day's breakfast and lunch. Carrie tried to draw him out, thanking him politely for the excellent stew. That pleased him. He said he had made it himself.

'Rabbit!' Mike exclaimed with relish.

He spat out a pellet and added:

'Shot with an air rifle.'

'Know a lot, don't you?' Screw replied sarcastically, and seemed a little uneasy.

'Do you often do a kidnapping?' Carrie asked with her mouth full. 'It must need such a lot of work to plan it all.'

'So it does. But they've got it down to a fine art in Italy.'

'Is that where you learned it?'

'Mind your own business!'

'Sorry! I didn't mean to ask questions. But it's so very cruel to us.'

'You'll get over it. Do you good! You'll see how the other half lives.'

'They don't live in a damp cellar in the dark,' Mike said.

'He means people like himself who want to get rich,' Carrie explained. 'Have you any children?'

'No, and don't want 'em.'

'Then you'll be glad to get rid of us. When are you going to let us go?'

'Tomorrow if you're lucky. Now you eat your food while I have a good look round!'

He flashed his lantern round their prison and began to walk through the archway which led to the second cellar. Terrified that he would spot the pile of bricks, they watched him helplessly. Carrie was the first to react. She stumbled towards the steps as if to escape through the open grating.

Screw rushed back and easily caught her before she reached the top.

'Thought you'd lock me in with your young friend, did you?' he exclaimed, marching her back to her place.

'Just to let you see how the other half lives.'

'None of your lip, baby!'

He grabbed her shoulders, shook her and threw her roughly down on her sleeping bag. She began to cry pitifully, saying that she was only a little girl; but the trick didn't work.

'And don't you try that one on me! No grub for you tomorrow morning!'

He picked up the bag containing their meagre breakfast and lunch, went up the stairs and bolted the grating.

'You couldn't possibly have made it in time,' Mike said.

'I know. I just wanted to stop him looking round the Powder Room.'

'Cor, that was clever! For a moment I was afraid you were going to leave me down here with him.'

'You know I wouldn't.'

'Well, I suppose I do now that I think about it. And the same goes for me, Carrie. I'm not leaving you alone.'

'Do you believe it's true that they'll send us home tomorrow?'

'I expect so. You were sure your Dad would pay up.'

'Then it doesn't matter if we miss breakfast.'

'Shall we go on with the bricks now?' Mike suggested.

'It doesn't seem worth the trouble if this is our last night here. But I tell you what – we'll put them all back loosely. Then nobody will ever notice.'

They both slept well, persuading themselves that

next day they would be home. When they woke up they knew it was morning from the grey streaks at the grating, but neither knew the time. Carrie had a tiny, very expensive watch which never worked but looked pretty on her wrist. Mike had a tough, cheap one which was always right, but in the excitement of the night before he had forgotten to wind it up. So they waited and waited, every ten minutes seeming at least an hour, but nobody came to fetch them. They had not even the heart to dance again to pass the time.

It must have been late in the afternoon when they heard steps above them and the unbolting of the grating. They were sure that this at last meant release since they were never visited during the day.

This time two masked men came down the stairs – Screw and a powerfully-built man whose black beard could just be distinguished. Mike said nothing. Carrie greeted them politely. Ignoring the children, Beard examined the cellar closely as if he wanted it for some other purpose than a prison. He stood in the archway flashing a torch all round the second cellar, but never spotted that there was anything wrong with the bricks. The two stood there talking in low voices and then prepared to leave.

'Are we going home now?' Carrie asked them at last.

'Not for a few days,' Screw answered.

'Oh! Well, can we have something to eat?'

'Not now. You must wait till it's dark.'

When they had gone, Carrie and Mike were very near to despair but neither was going to be the first to break down.

'And I couldn't hear a thing they said!' Carrie complained.

'I could – just a very little. They were standing near a pillar and the sound came down on my side like a whisper.'

'Was he Italian, the man with the beard?'

'I don't think so. Nothing wrong with his English. Perhaps it was over there that he learned to kidnap.'

'What did you hear?'

'Not a lot. Something about police and a photograph and my mother being comforted, and then it faded out except at the end of a long bit of talking by Beard when I think he said: "never be found".'

'I don't like it, Mike.'

'Nor do I. And I'm hungry. Well, let's get on with the bricks. I wish we had done some this morning.'

'Better wait till Screw has brought our supper. He might go in there again.'

It was long after dark when he arrived. He did not come down, but opened the grating and tossed their food on to the top stair, telling them to fetch it and slamming home the bolt. He had not gone to any trouble for them this time. No stew, no cocoa. Just a loaf of bread and a hunk of cheese.

They ate it all ravenously and then returned to the half-moon of brickwork. When the pile of bricks was again back on the floor, Mike began picking away at the inner courses which were now laid bare. The mortar was not so rotten and the job harder. When his hands were tired, Carrie took over and it was she who broke through into the emptiness behind.

'Nothing!' she exclaimed, disappointed. 'Nothing but blackness!'

'Well, we thought it couldn't be solid. Let's have a look!'

There was nothing to look at, only a brick-sized slice of night. He put his ear to the hole. There was no sound, or not more than if he had listened to a big sea shell.

Mike took over and pulled out eight bricks from two courses – a useful hole but still revealing nothing. When he put his arm through and tried to light the darkness with a candle, it flickered and went out. All he could see was that they had broken into a round shaft which looked like a well. He threw down half a brick and heard it splash at the bottom of the shaft. That clinched it. A well it was.

'There must be an opening at the top,' he told Carrie, 'but I don't see how we can ever get up there.'

'Let's make the hole big enough to get through, and then wait till there's some light.'

'All right. Want to have a go?'

Carrie took the knife and did her best, but her fingers were not so toughened as those of a farmer's son. They had been blistered by her earlier work and now were nearly raw flesh. She showed them to Mike in the light of the candle.

'Oh, blast the bricks!' he exclaimed, and gave them a furious kick more out of pity for her than frustration.

The result was a zig-zagging crack running up from the floor to the side of the small hole they had made. Mike took hold of the top course and shook it, pressing inwards with his feet. A solid chunk of bricks came away into the cellar and more splashed into the well. They could now enter the shaft with ease, but all was still blackness and the candle was running low.

'We'll go to bed now and get up at the crack of dawn,' Mike said. 'Keep an eye on the grating whenever you turn over and wake me as soon as it's light. And I'll bring my bag over to your side of the cellar so that I can see the grating too.'

Consequently sleep was very broken. Once Carrie, half dreaming, said it was morning when it wasn't. Once Mike, feeling that the night was far too long, decided that the steps and the grating were not where he thought they were and lit the candle to find out; they had not moved and it was still night. After that he slept soundly until Carrie nudged him and said:

'I can just see the stair.'

No doubt about it. The light was growing somewhere above them. They quickly finished up the last of the dry bread and felt their way into the second cellar. The inside of the shaft was definitely lighter than it had been at night; they could see upwards but not downwards. The well seemed to be closed at the top. At some time in the past, however, it had been open, for an iron ladder was clamped to the bricks nearly within reach.

'I think I can get a hand to it if you hang on to my feet,' Mike said.

'But how will you get back?'

'Same way. I'll stretch out an arm and you grab my wrist with both hands.'

Carrie sat on his legs while he wriggled on his

stomach over the edge, twisted and grabbed the upright of the ladder.

'Got it! You can let go now.'

'But is it safe?'

'It seems quite firm. Why shouldn't it be? I'll go up and see if we can make a way out at the top.'

Mike swung himself on to the ladder and climbed up. It ended at a height hardly more than the height of the cellar. Two great beams crossed the top of the shaft and on top of them were paving stones. One of them had tilted where a big root had knocked out supporting bricks on the rim of the well. A little light came through the hole and the slight gap between the stones. One could probably break through given a pick-axe and something solid underfoot, but from the ladder it was impossible – nor would anyone dare to bring down a slab of stone while standing underneath.

'I'll go down to the bottom now,' he said.

'I wish you'd come back,' Carrie answered nervously. 'There can't be anything at the bottom and it's all no good.'

'Well, you never know. Suppose there was a drain half way down big enough for us to get through. Light a new candle, Carrie, and pass it out to me!'

The candle burned clearly, for there was plenty of fresh air now that they had opened up the hole. Mike went down, always carefully feeling every rung of the ladder before he put his weight on it and never letting go with his free hand till he was sure. He had been taught that while helping his father to prune overgrown apple trees.

Far down he came to the inky black level of the

water. It was quite still, though after he had watched it for a minute he detected a slight rise and fall. He had the impression that it was deep. Bitterly disappointed that all their work and hopes had come to nothing, he began to climb up again. Neither at top nor bottom was there any way out of the shaft.

He was not far from the hole and Carrie's helping hand when the topmost clamps of the ladder pulled out from the well-head. A brick whizzed past his head and another glanced off his shoulder. The ladder leaned out from the wall under his weight, then crashed into the other side of the shaft. One of the uprights broke; the other slowly bent while he watched it in horror. Then it cracked and he hurtled down the well, conscious of nothing but his terrible speed, but remembering to draw a deep breath before he hit the water.

Carrie, too appalled to utter a word, watched Mike swing from the bending section of ladder and saw it break. The sound of his plunge to the bottom rolled and echoed up the shaft. She called again and again, but there was no answer. Far down the ripples and suckings of the unseen water died away and all was silent.

She ran to the steps and screamed for help, knowing all the time that her voice would never be heard. Then she returned to the hole they had made, talking to the darkness and listening in case Mike had come to the surface and found something to hang on to. At last she lay down on her sleeping bag, numbed and shocked by the death of her dear companion. It was a long time before she began to shed tears which went on and on.

Later in the morning or perhaps the afternoon – she

only knew that it was not yet night – she heard foot-steps above. Again two men were coming. She rushed to the top of the steps and called wildly to them to be quick, and that there had been an accident. She knew that it was far too late to rescue Mike, but perhaps there was something which grown men could do.

Beard and Screw opened the grating and came down. Incoherently she began to explain what had happened. They did not listen to more than the first few words and went straight into the second cellar while she followed behind begging them to help.

They looked into the hole and saw the broken ladder.

'Poor little bastard!' Screw said casually.

'They don't understand risks at that age,' Beard remarked. 'Well, it saves us trouble.'

For the moment Carrie could not see what trouble it could possibly save them.

'Can't you do anything?' she implored them. 'Isn't there any way you can get down?'

They ignored her completely.

'Are you able to get hold of some mortar, boss?' Screw asked.

'The gardener has some for repairs to the ruins.'

'Then I'll build that up again tonight.'

'Not yet. The well might be useful.'

'Blasted newspapers! Can't keep their noses out of anything!'

'Well, if it wasn't for the photograph, we'd never have known that Falconer had gone to the police.'

'Haven't you – haven't you got the money for me?' Carrie asked.

'No, sweetie, we haven't,' Beard answered.

'It will come. I know it will come.'

'So will Christmas.'

'Please may I have another candle? I'm so afraid now in this darkness.'

She dreaded the coming night when she would be alone again. Clearly the kidnappers' plans had gone wrong. They seemed almost glad that Mike was dead and she was sure they no longer cared what happened to her. She loathed the cold way in which Beard called her 'sweetie'.

'I haven't any more,' Beard replied. 'He'll stay here with the lantern while you eat your supper.'

'I don't want any. I couldn't eat.'

'As you like.'

'What's the time?' she asked.

'About three.'

'Did you hear me? Why did you come so early?'

'To see how to arrange things, sweetie. We know now.'

They went up and shut the grating. Carrie huddled into her bag and pulled Mike's nearer to her for comfort. She fell into an exhausted sleep, and when she woke up the dim, grey light had turned to the velvet blackness of a grave.

4

The Path of the Water

Mike hit the water legs first, went straight to the bottom and fell over on to sand. Instantly he was swirled sideways and jammed under something solid which felt like stone. A current rushed past him as he fought to free himself and rise to the surface, but all his struggles only resulted in freeing his legs while the upper part of his body remained stuck in a slot. He tried to push himself back and stretched out his arms for something to shove against. The straightening of arms and streamlining of his slight body did the trick. The water carried him forwards under the sill. When he felt that his legs were clear he gave a kick to shoot himself to the surface. To his amazement he found that his legs touched bottom and he could stand with the fast-running stream only up to his waist.

He coughed the water out of his lungs and very cautiously waded on through the unseen, feeling his way with his hands protecting his head. Sometimes he could stand upright; sometimes he had to bend; and once the stream deepened so that it was easier to swim a few strokes than to walk. After the panic which had seized him when he was trapped under the sill he was empty of fear and bewildered that he could be alive.

Shivering with cold, he stumbled on until the passage became lower than ever. He was up to his chest in the stream, and the roof just above his head. As he ran his hands over it he could feel wide cracks. Once from the edge of such a fissure he knocked down a long sliver of rock. When he had passed it he heard a shower of stones behind him – a warning that the whole passage could be horribly unsafe.

A little further on he had proof of it. Here a great chunk of the tunnel roof had collapsed. At the top of the dome left by the fall he could see a small, ragged triangle of sky, far out of reach. The fall had completely blocked the channel, piling up the water which foamed under it and leaving no easy way through or over for him.

For the moment he was content just to use his eyes again. He sat down on a heap of boulders and gravel, drawing deep breaths of gladness and fresh air as he looked up at the patch of blue. Now that he could at last see around him, the whole scene of his escape was no longer such a mystery.

Long ago – many centuries ago to judge by the church-like arches of the cellar – men had discovered the underground water and dug a well to tap it, starting at the level where he and Carrie had been imprisoned. Then they must have decided that it was inconvenient to go up and down stairs to fetch water, so they built up the brick casing and made a new well-head higher up. Later on, the well was closed altogether by the beams and paving stones which he had seen. He knew a lot about wells, having watched fascinated the clearing of the old well at home and the sinking of a new one.

As for the sill under which he had been swept, he

could understand that too. At the bottom of the well they had made an outlet much narrower than the inlet so that the level of water was always high. In winter floods it might come nearly up to the floor of the cellar; in drought the stream perhaps ran straight through without piling up in the well at all.

Now able to guess at the 'why' of everything he was a lot more hopeful than when his world had been a nightmare of darkness with no sense in it. If the water somewhere flowed into the open there was a chance that he could make his way out with it. But first he had to climb the blockage.

The main mass of fallen roof was a huge slab of solid stone. The sheer face was overhanging a pile of broken rock and rubble. A grown man might perhaps have reached some sort of handhold and climbed it, but Mike could not. The only hope was to build a rough platform on which to stand.

He began to roll loose rocks down the channel and lift them into position. The job was interminable, and soon his arms were too tired to do any more heaving. He nearly gave up, for there was no telling how far he would have to go and if at the end of it all he could escape. He was tempted to return into the well though he knew it would be quite impossible against the rush of water.

Standing there hopelessly, he suddenly noticed that he had an unexpected result from all his work. His wretched, unfinished platform had dammed one of the channels through which the stream was running under the slab; it was now flowing along the side of the tunnel and rapidly sweeping away a bar of earth and gravel. In a little while he heard a growl of pebbles and a crunch as the whole mass, its support worn away, abruptly shifted sideways.

Mike jumped back in alarm and waited for disaster, but the unsteady lump of limestone had come to rest, leaving a narrow chimney between its side and the wall of the tunnel. It could be climbed with knees and elbows so long as the slab did not move another few inches and squash him.

He wriggled nervously up to the top and found that the rock was lying with its downstream end much lower than the other, giving plenty of room to pass under the roof. The black tunnel beyond was higher than it had been, free of all but scattered rocks. Though he could not even see the water, the stream seemed to be deeper and running more slowly. He had no idea of time or distance. Since his fall from the ladder he might have travelled a mile or only a few hundred yards.

At last the darkness was suffused with a greenish pallor in which he could see – but as little as at the bottom of a deep dive in a cloudy river. Further on the light became clearer until he stopped and stared at the dreamy, mermaid beauty of the scene before him. The stream had spread out into a deep pool. The green radiance was coming from a point under water at the far end, reflected by smooth rock. Higher up the specks of shell in the limestone sparkled like dark emeralds.

It was the gate to freedom. He waded in and took to swimming when nearly out of his depth. Over the green light a current tended to drag him down, so he clawed his way out of it along the rock and tried to make up his mind what to do. Without a doubt this was the outlet where the water bubbled to the surface as a powerful spring; and if it was like other springs there would be a number of separate openings, none of them large enough to let him through. But all of them had to be tried.

Mike drew several deep breaths and dived for the light. Under water he could see the openings and a scatter of sunshine in the outer world. There was one and only one possible route if a big, round boulder could be shifted. He lay on the gravel like a spawning salmon, clinging to it with both arms. Twisting and turning, he tried to drag it back with his feet against rock, and could not clear it. But again the water helped him. When he had to let go, the boulder rolled a little forward.

He came up for air and dived at the stone, kicking with all the strength he had left. It rolled once more and settled for ever, firmly jammed between solid rock above and below. The stream carried him with it through the wider passage. He stuck, but now it was only mud and pebbles which held his shoulders; one heave, and he was floundering in another and shallower pool surrounded by trees. The blessed sun, which for four days he had not seen, patterned the water with the shadow of branches, and that grim, buried stream rippled and raced downhill as if it had innocently sprung from nowhere.

It was a gloriously hot day. By the sun he reckoned that it was a bit after midday and four or five hours had passed since he fell down the well. His first thought was to rush off for help, but he could not do it. He was

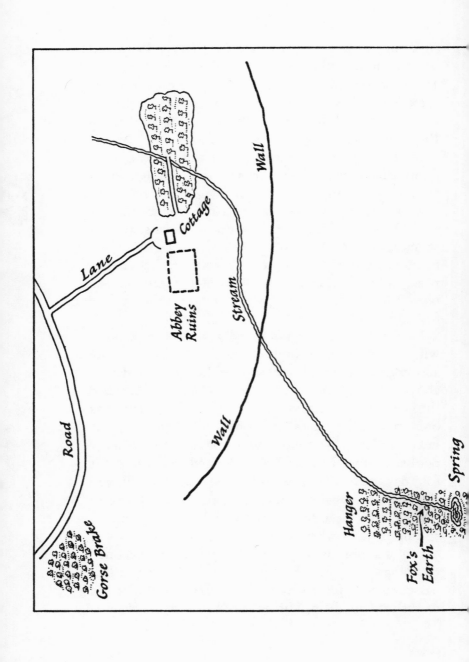

shivering uncontrollably and his knees would not hold him up any longer. The very first necessity was to get warm again. So he struggled out of his clothes and tumbled them on to a blackberry bush to dry. For himself he found a warm, flat patch of bare rock in full sun above the spring, and there he collapsed.

There was no guessing in what part of silent England he was. The copse of hazel and mixed timber might be anywhere. He hoped that someone would appear and that he could tell his story, but nobody did; nor was there any sound of life on the land – no cattle or sheep, no voices, no rattle of a tractor. It did not look like mountain country but it must be fairly wild. A big hawk, which he believed was a peregrine, sailed overhead. In the afternoon he saw a vixen playing with her cubs before she scented him.

That brought him back to life. He had toasted both sides again and again and was warm. His clothes were not yet dry, so he turned them and spread them out on the thorns. Staying in cover, he followed the stream down to the edge of the trees and found himself on the lower slope of a hillside with another hillside opposite and patches of woodland in the valley. There were no houses anywhere near, but he could see the grey, square tower of a village church in the distance. The copse was what they called a hanger – a strip of beech, fir and hazel running directly down the hill.

He returned to his clothes and put them on. They were not so dry as his mother would have liked, but would be good enough after another hour of sun. Then he pushed his way up through the hazels, passing the fox's earth on the way. The mouth of it was so wide and worn that generations of them must have lived there, and probably badgers too.

From the top of the hanger he saw rolling downland with no visible villages. Sheep country it was, and here and there were the white dots of them on the turf. About half a mile away, out in the open except for a wood alongside it, were a cottage and some ruins. Remains of windows and archways suggested that it had been a church. That must be where Carrie and he had been held. The cellar beneath it was, he remembered, known as a crypt.

Right! So the thing to do was to run down immediately to the village with the church tower and get help. He hesitated, thinking it out while he looked at the square of walls which cut the skyline. Tourists must surely visit the ruins. The crypt was in perfect condition and probably interesting to people who liked that kind of thing. They couldn't be kept out, for it was not dangerous with crumbling stonework like the dungeon he had been shown. Suppose some teacher came along with a party of children? The teacher would go yarning away about history and architecture, and all of them would want to see the crypt. So it was not a safe prison at all. There must be another underground building which nobody knew about, either very deep down or some distance away so that visitors would hear nothing however loudly Carrie and he yelled for help.

It was then that he remembered the missing bullock. In his district farmers had been having trouble with cattle rustlers, just as in the Wild West, but not on horseback. Men drove up to an outlying field in a truck, chose a good beast, shot it and loaded it. One night his father and some friends had nearly caught the thieves. They heard a truck drive off in a hurry, but all they ever saw were two men walking innocently along a bridle path against whom nothing could be proved.

Next day a fine Angus steer was missing, to be discovered a week later tipped out into a ditch and carefully covered. What had happened was obvious. The rustlers had killed it but had to escape before they could load it.

All this excitement had made a deep impression on Mike – especially after seeing the poor, rotting bullock. He could imagine something of the sort happening up there at the ruins. The kidnappers would see the police coming and just walk off in different directions as harmless hikers. But they could not take Carrie with them.

He himself could never guide the police to her. Then what was the chance of her being found? Of course, she would be found in time, but it might be too long a time. It took a week before his father's nose had led him to that bullock.

He was very much afraid for Carrie. He was sure that Beard had used the words 'never be found'. It seemed unbelievable that they would let her die just because they couldn't get money for her, but he had read of such things in the papers. People did kill rather than risk going to prison for a long time. And how easy it would be with that yawning hole in the second cellar! Down she might go at the first hint of police and nobody would suspect those casual tourists walking far away in the distance.

So he decided that the most urgent task was to find out where Carrie was while the kidnappers were still confident that nobody had any clue to her whereabouts. As soon as they visited her and saw the well they would be quite sure that he was dead and that they had nothing to fear from him. They might, he thought with a bit of a shudder, even be mighty glad. If there was any risk of being seen and caught by them, he would have to run for it and run fast.

Between the hanger and the cluster of ruins, cottage and wood a long, dry-stone wall curved along the slope, one end disappearing behind the wood, the other running up to a point which was high enough to give him a full view. In spite of the bare, open hillside he believed he could reach the cover of the wall crawling from patches of nettle to dips in the ground.

He ducked behind the wall, still apparently unseen, and followed it up until he overlooked the site of the ancient church. There was not much still standing except a square with archways in it. The rest was mainly lawns and isolated masses of masonry. Foundation walls and stone pavements had been cleared so that the ground plan was clear as on a map. If their prison was underneath, the way in should be easy to find.

The cottage was beyond the ruins, out in the open and close to a small car park with a single lane leading to it. So far as he could see there was no car or van near it and no garage. He thought again of the men he had imagined who could stroll off on foot if any danger threatened with nothing suspicious about them.

Food was only brought at night. That suggested to Mike that Screw could not risk moving about by day when visitors might arrive at any moment to look at the ruins. Probably he walked over from the cottage; he must have cooked that rabbit stew somewhere. The best plan was to creep up in the dusk, watch where he went with Carrie's food and follow him closely. When he had come up from underground and gone away it should not be hard to find the grating. Then he and Carrie, safely together, could run down to the village with the church tower and see that the police surrounded the ruins before dawn.

He tried to remember when he had last seen the moon and what shape it was. Yes, on Friday night from his bedroom window, and it had been a bit bigger than the half. So it should be full moon that night or the next, and in a clear sky if the weather held. What a waste to have been underground for four lovely days in a summer which had had few of them! Anyway he could count on seeing whatever moved at over a hundred yards.

Mike had always been a hunter in his small way. His father had taught him to shoot – though he was too young to be allowed a gun of his own – and Great-uncle Jim had taught him to pick up a meal without any gun at all. Jim was now seventy years old and had been a gamekeeper in his time. He knew every poacher's trick and snare there were, and it amused him to pass them on down another two generations – on condition that his pupil promised never to try them on anyone else's land without permission. The result was that Mike during autumn week-ends would be missing all day and would come proudly home after dusk with a couple of rabbits and occasionally a hare or a pheasant.

So he knew how to move without being heard and to see without being seen. The kidnappers were certainly townsmen – he was sure of that, though exactly how he knew it he could not have said – and he was confident that their eyes would not be so keen as a wood pigeon's or their ears as good as those of an old buck rabbit.

He waited patiently behind the wall and at dusk started for the ruins. A brilliant full moon rose. so that the church walls were black and white as an over-exposed photograph. As long as he stuck to the patches of black he was invisible. Lights went on in the cottage and stayed on. He hoped that someone was making hot stew for poor Carrie. Whatever they were doing, it was reassuring to know that from the inside of the cottage nothing could be seen of the outside.

However, it was not safe to assume that they were all in the cottage at the same time. Carrie and he, after comparing notes, were sure that there were three of them. Slinking from shadow, he entered the ruins. Stuck in the grass close to the cottage was a notice board with raised white letters easily read in the moonlight:

SITE OF HILCOTE ABBEY
National Trust Property
Open to the Public 10 a.m.–6.30 p.m.

This was followed by a short note of the history of the Abbey, from which he gathered that it had been built in 1146, suppressed by Henry VIII in 1539, then deserted and on its wild site half forgotten till little remained but tumbled stones overgrown by trees and bushes. The ruins had been cleared in 1906. Well, Mike thought, they might believe they had cleared all of them but they hadn't.

All the time he watched the cottage, expecting somebody to come out with food for Carrie; but nobody did. Perhaps the entrance to the crypt was actually inside the cottage? It seemed most unlikely. There was always a risk of visitors dropping in to ask questions or buy postcards, and how could the kidnappers be so sure that cries for help would never be heard?

Mike left the ruins and very cautiously inspected the cottage. On the side facing the grey expanse of the car park there was no cover; on the other side were a low hedge, a bit of garden and the lit window. This was more promising. The edge of the wood was fairly close. He could escape into it if he was caught peeping through the window or listening. At least he hoped he could. That depended on how fast they could run and what obstacles were in the way.

So first he entered the wood and found a path running through it to the cottage. That gave him more confidence. If he were spotted and chased he could swerve off the path into dark trees and would take some finding.

He was still on the path when he heard voices approaching, which allowed him time to lie down in long grass and listen. Two men were strolling over to the cottage. One of them was Screw. The other was the very respectable driver who had pretended to Carrie that he was a studio chauffeur and to Mike that he was a film director; so it must be the man with the beard who was in the cottage and had turned on the light.

He heard a scrap of their conversation as they came towards him and passed. Screw said:

'She didn't want any supper, so why bother?'

'A bit hard,' Chauffeur replied, 'but what does it matter?'

'Anyway, I don't want to see her again if I can help it.'

'Yes. Leave it to him!'

Mike could not help understanding what they meant. He told himself that it was his imagination, that he must be wrong, that nobody would do such a thing. Following the two at a safe distance, he saw them enter the cottage and then crept up under the lit window where there was a strip of earth between the wall and a low, untidy hedge of box. He lay with his body stretched full length huddled in the angle. It was in black shadow, and his clothes, covered by dried mud, were dark as the earth. He reckoned that nobody would ever see him unless opening the window and looking directly down.

One of them did open the window. He thought that was the end. He did not even dare to dig in his toes for a wild jump away.

'God, it's hot! And what a fug!' Chauffeur said.

'You'll have the moths in,' Screw's voice remarked.

'Well, we'll be out of here tomorrow.'

Voices turned away from the window, and Mike heard the splash of something in a glass. Then one of them asked:

'What did you decide, boss? Wall it up?'

'No,' Beard replied. 'Why give them the clue of fresh mortar if it's ever found? First thing tomorrow we'll remove the grating and put a flag-stone in its place. I've found the right size. It will never be noticed.'

'You're not going to just leave her?' Chauffeur asked.

'No. The way the boy went.'

Mike hunched himself backwards till he was clear of the window and could stand up. Before stepping over the hedge he brushed out his footprints with his hand. Those they might notice, but it was a hundred to one against anyone spotting that the earth beneath the window was flatter than it ought to be.

Again his first impulse was to run for the police, but he was more than ever obsessed by the thought that the kidnappers would escape at the first sight of car head-lights approaching and that Carrie might never be found even if she was still alive. He could not guide the police. He had not the remotest idea where the hidden entrance to the crypt could be.

Yet only he could rescue her quickly and silently. Could he get back up the watercourse and under the sill? But he had long ago decided it was impossible. And even if it could be done would Carrie jump and would they both have the astonishing luck to be carried through before they drowned? Anyway it was lunacy to try the double journey when he remembered the deadly cold of his passage underground. His strength had so nearly given out.

The stream would lead him back to the cellar and its well if there were any means of telling its hidden course from the surface. The rock fall might help. It was prob-ably about the middle of the hanger not far from the fox's earth, but among thick bushes a mere dip in the ground would be hard to find at night. He could be sure of nothing except that the stream was not very far underground.

That brought to mind the culvert which carried a muddy brook under the drive to his father's farm. The culvert? It might be possible, after all, to know the course of the stream. That twig between his hands had jumped all right when crossing the culvert.

It had happened during the drought of the previous summer. The farm always had ample water for men and beasts, pumped up by an electric ram. But in August the well began to run dry, so they had it cleaned out and the water analysed. The report from the county laboratory announced that it was quite unfit to drink.

Both his parents had been very worried. Mr Prowse insisted that he had always drunk the water and his father and grandfather before him, and that none of them was ever one penny the worse. Mrs Prowse retorted that what with home-made cider and all that beer they never drank any water anyway, and what would he think of himself if she and Mike were pushing up the daisies in the churchyard?

So his father had to buy drinking water from tankers until one day Mrs Prowse said:

'You always used to be talking about dowsers and how they found water for the army when you were a soldier in the Western Desert. If you know there's something in it, why don't you try one?'

Jack Prowse jumped at it. He telephoned a professional dowser who came out to the farm in a more expensive car than they themselves could afford and walked all over their land with a steel spring between his hands. On the Upper Ley he told the Prowses that they would find water at twenty feet and that his firm would pipe it down to the house at a reasonable price. No water, no pay.

Mike's mother was a bit doubtful, as she usually was when she had started something up and her husband had grown too enthusiastic about it.

'Try it for yourself, Mrs Prowse!' the dowser had said. 'Some people can't feel it at all. Most can feel it a little. And a few can do it well straight off. I'll cut a hazel fork for you.'

He cut a twig of springy hazel in the shape of a Y and showed them how to hold down the forked part between the palms of both hands.

'Now walk along the drive over that culvert,' he said, 'and see what happens!'

Jack Prowse was disappointed that he could feel nothing at all. Janet said she thought the fork moved but couldn't be sure. And in Mike's hands the stem of the Y twisted up so quickly that it startled him.

So the trick was worth trying, there in the moonlight, as a last chance. It could show him the course of the water and lead him to the well beneath the ruins. Mike hurried back to the top edge of the hanger and cut and trimmed a fork of hazel in the way he remembered.

Choosing a rough line between the ruins and the spring, he walked slowly across it. The fork seemed to twist between his hands, but he was trembling a little and refused to trust it. He recrossed the line further on and this time there was no doubt. The stem of the hazel twig jumped through a half circle like the needle on a dial.

He trotted on fast over the open ground, testing for water at intervals and then not bothering, since the line was running straight for the Abbey. When he reached the outskirts of the ruins he crossed the unseen line again to be sure of the direction of the well. The fork did not move. He went along the whole length of the Abbey. It still did not move. He had lost the water.

Fearing all the time that the gift had suddenly left him, he passed across the back of the cottage. The light was still on and he could hear voices, so there was no need for caution. He carried out a thorough search in case the cellar was after all under the floor of the building; but still nothing.

Sitting down at a safe distance he thought and thought, trying to remember if there had been a sharp turn in the passage underground. He was sure that he had never gone round a corner, but in the pitch darkness he would never have noticed a slight curve. He found that he did not much like retracing that horrible journey in memory. It made him shiver again.

And then at last he had it. Tree roots in the second cellar! Tree roots, of course! On his route over the surface there had not been a tree, and there wasn't one in the cottage garden or the ruins, so the stream must run under the wood. He walked round outside it. Nothing was wrong with the hazel fork or with him. It jumped as if it were impatient, and at once he was into the trees, crossing and recrossing the line every few yards so as not to lose it again.

The underground water led him over the path through the wood and out the other side of it. There he stopped. For the first time it occurred to him that the fork could lead him for miles to the source of the water, but could never tell him where the well was. All he knew was that it was somewhere under trees.

He tried to recall the number of arches between the steps in the first cellar and the well at the end of the second, and came to the conclusion that the distance would be about thirty yards; but that was no help to finding the entrance. There on the surface it was impossible to say whether the steps were to the right or left of the well. He remembered keenly how Carrie, when they first met in the dark, muddled right and left because she did not know which way his head was pointing.

He returned to the path through the wood, followed it up away from the line of the water and then froze. In a clearing were two black mounds. Stalking them very warily through the undergrowth he found that they were two pup tents. He crept up closer. They were empty. Outside was a Primus stove, a frying pan and the earthenware pot in which the soup and the rabbit stew had been. Obviously this was where Screw and Chauffeur were camping. The instinct which had led him to believe that in any danger they could walk off innocently was quite correct. With pup tents and gear packed on their backs nobody would dream that they were anything but poor and cheerful tourists with a taste for old churches.

Now there was real hope; he might be able to tell which way Screw had walked from the tents whenever he was not on the path to the cottage. The most promising track was an opening in the bushes which went nowhere in particular, but he could find no hole or depression in the ground. Another led to a rubbish pit. There he wasted still more time clearing cans and stale bread, and came on nothing but bare earth underneath. A third track, just distinguishable on the moonlit grass, led into the open on the edge of the wood.

It seemed too far from the line of the water, but the low bank and shallow ditch which bordered the wood looked worth exploring. A large stone, shining white, caught his eye. Perhaps there had once been a wall, not the usual hedge and ditch between trees and the open. He poked a stick into the bank. It had never been a hedge; it was the remains of a wall hidden under grass.

Walking along it he came on a pile of dead brush-wood leaning against the bank which did not look natural. The wood was untidy and uncared for; even in moonlight he could see that nobody had been cutting or clearing for years. He pulled to one side a dead branch which was not entangled with the rest and easily moved. Under it was a hole with a bundle of bramble shoved into it. That too was easily pulled out in one piece. He still was not sure, but when he ran his hands over the straight sides of the hole he found solid masonry not loose stones. That could not be part of a field wall built on the surface; it was a massive thing with its foundations far below ground. When he sat down and slid in legs foremost, his feet at once met a step-ladder. After reaching out to pull the bramble more or less back into position, he descended into the darkness, wildly excited by his success.

5

Dawn of Freedom

Almost at once Mike realised that success was still far away. He was back in that absolute blackness where he could not even see his hands. This was an outlying bit of the Abbey all right, for there was the same sort of paving underfoot. Roof and timber walls had evidently fallen down centuries ago; turf and leaf mould had then covered the debris, leaving beneath the surface hollows and passages wherever tree roots or stone footings prevented complete collapse. Crawling under beams and over rubble, he found the remains of wooden pillars, not stone, and piles of what felt like rotten straw, showing that the roof had been thatched. In one place he was tied up among partitions of decayed timber. He worked his way in and out of them, completely puzzled until he recognised that he was in a range of stables and that the whole buried building had been a barn.

To find the grating and the steps which led down to the cellars was going to be nearly impossible. All he knew was that the course of the stream lay to the left of the entrance and its ladder. He was still near enough to them to find his way back, and he then followed the main wall, feeling his way along the tunnel between solid stone and piles of rubbish. He stopped every few paces to hold the hazel fork between his palms, but it seemed as blind and lost as he was.

At last the fork jumped, its stem describing a complete circle. He left the wall and kept to the line of the underground water, shuffling forward very nervously into nothingness. The only hope was to find that blocked well-head by touch and work away from it. Something like a snake brushed his face and made him start back. He dabbed at it with a shaky hand and found that it was a thin, hanging root attached to a much bigger one which had crawled down from the trees above him. He knelt and ran his hands over the floor. A paving stone was tilted. The root was alongside it. The rough line of mortar was curved, not straight. All these fitted the appearance of the well-head as he had seen it from below.

Now for the worst of it – to strike out away from the water for thirty yards with no guidance at all from eyes or fork. He hoped the line of the old posts would keep him going straight, but their stumps were often missing or could not be found among the rubble. He was soon helplessly lost. The count of paces had gone wrong and he was sure that he had moved diagonally across from one line of posts to another. All he could do was to shout and keep on shouting for Carrie and pray that he couldn't be heard on the surface if the two men had returned to their tents.

He could not recognise his voice, sometimes muffled by closed, soft spaces, sometimes echoing from an unseen wall and whining away into mysterious distance. There was no reply. He moved about at random and called:

'Carrie! Carrie, where are you?'

At last, very faintly, coming from nowhere, he heard an answer.

'Don't hurt me, Mike! Don't hurt me!'

'Of course I won't hurt you,' he shouted. 'Show a light at the grating if you can!'

'It's really you?'

'Of course it's me!'

'I thought you were . . . I thought . . .'

'Well, I wouldn't have hurt you anyway.'

'I've only matches,' she said.

'Come up the steps and strike one after another under the grating!'

He kept turning round and staring but could see nothing.

'Set fire to a whole pile of them!'

Much further away than he expected he saw a glow and felt his way towards it. He slid back the bolt and opened the grating. Carrie caught his hands and stayed in his arms trembling.

'How are you alive?' she asked.

'I got out at the bottom into a stream. Tell you all about it later. And I came in through the hole in the wall that Screw uses. But I don't know how to find it again.'

Only two matches were left. She struck one. It was little help, for it showed only a stump, a roof beam and nothing beyond. The last match wouldn't strike at all.

The disappointment finished Mike. He felt suddenly exhausted. He had done what he set out to do, and that was that. All the courage and effort turned out to be useless.

'Why can't we just walk until we hit a wall? Then if we follow it we must find where you got in.'

'You don't know what it's like, Carrie. At night we

could go round and round for ever and still miss the ladder and the hole.'

'Well, we can't wait for daylight. Suppose someone came down?'

Mike remembered that Beard intended to do so. The chance of getting out before they were picked up by the light of his lantern was slim. Carrie said:

'I remember which way the footsteps used to come – from the right. Let's start off that way!'

They set off hand in hand. After a while Carrie tripped over the grating. They had gone round in a circle while sure they were going straight.

'Now you see,' Mike said.

'Up here is it like it was down below?'

'No. I think this was a great barn with a cellar underneath for wine and anything that had to be stored a long time. And it belonged to the Abbey.'

'What Abbey?'

'That's where we are. In the ruins of an old Abbey. But the barn just had posts instead of arches and pillars. There may be two lines of stumps down the middle.'

Carrie let go his hand.

'You stay here and I'll find one of them,' she said. 'Then you come to my voice, and we'll go on doing it in turn until we arrive at an outside wall.'

She slipped away, hit a stump fairly quickly and hit it hard.

'Hurt yourself?' Mike asked.

'Only my knee. Now I'll keep talking and you come to me.'

Her plan at least prevented them from going round in a circle, but since they could not tell which way they were facing they must often have returned to the same post. However, eventually they reached the face of an outside wall.

'Right or left to get to the entrance?' she asked.

'Oh, how do I know?' he cried in despair. 'I can't tell what wall I came in by. And I'm getting awfully tired and cold again, Carrie. I've had nothing to eat since the bread and cheese yesterday.'

'Then we'll sit still for a bit,' she said. 'Put on my poncho, Mike, and lie down next to me!'

He went to sleep, but she could not. To know he was alive and that she would no longer be alone in that unmeaning darkness was like waking up from a monstrous dream. She was full of hope that in a few hours she would be home again, telling herself that as soon as they got out there must be people about to whom they could appeal for help. Mike had said something about the countryside around the Abbey ruins being very empty, but after all it was not in the middle of a desert.

She kept an arm over him to make sure he was always there and closed her eyes. Though it made no difference whether they were open or shut, it was comforting to know that the darkness belonged to her, not to this hell.

She dozed off and woke with a start, ashamed of herself. It was her duty to be on watch and to warn Mike if she heard one of the kidnappers coming down. She listened and stared all round. Something was different. In the distance there was a blackness which had a shape; it seemed to run diagonally between floor and roof. She woke up Mike. It took him a moment to distinguish what she was looking at.

'It's a bit of fallen roof, Carrie, and it's dawn outside. Dawn! We shall see the way out. Quick, before anyone comes!'

They stumbled over rubble towards the shadowy shape. An oak post had slipped sideways and cracked. The heavy beam above it was bent in the centre, and over it the roof sagged like slack canvas of a tent. Light came through the fractures – enough to explain why, during the day, they could make out the grating above them while they were imprisoned in the cellar.

Mike climbed over a tumble of earth and stone, very careful to disturb nothing, and then at last saw the entrance showing grey-blue through the black web of its plug of bramble.

'Don't make a sound!' he whispered. 'Two of them are in tents not far away and they mightn't be asleep.'

He went up the step-ladder, pushed away the bunch of bramble and came out on the glorious green of the bank. Carrie followed, and as he bent to help her out his foot slipped and he crashed into the pile of dead brushwood.

The two froze and listened. A wood pigeon took off from its roost with a clatter of wings followed by a dozen others rocketing through branches. A pair of magpies broke the silence with a loud chatter of protest at being woken up too early. They heard one of the campers crawling out of his tent. He appeared at the edge of the wood, saw nobody, exclaimed, 'Those blasted birds!' and returned.

When all was quiet Mike and Carrie tip-toed along the bank, taking cover again before they came within sight of the cottage.

'I think Beard may come out very soon,' Mike said, 'and then we can safely go past the cottage and put the ruins between us and them.'

'Why do you think he'll be up so early?'

'Just something I overheard.'

There was no reason to tell her that she had been so near to never being seen again.

And near she was, for only five minutes later Beard emerged from the cottage and took the path down the centre of the wood to the clearing where his two assistants had their tents.

As soon as they were sure that they were out of his sight, they dashed across the short stretch of open ground and put the cottage between themselves and the wood. As they passed the front, Carrie boldly tried the door. It was not locked.

'Wait till I get you something to eat!' she said. 'I'll grab the first thing I see in the kitchen.'

Mike crouched down behind the garden hedge, keeping an eye on the wood. He remembered that they had not replaced the grating. If Beard went down at once, it would not take him more than a minute to see that Carrie had escaped. What would they all do then? Clear out quick, he hoped, after spending a few minutes arguing about it. Beard was bound to believe that one of his men had forgotten to bolt the grating.

Carrie ran out of the cottage with the knuckle end of a ham, a loaf and two bottles of milk. They circled the car park, raced through the ruins and then had to decide what was their surest route to safety. Mike wanted to take to the open grassland which he had crossed in the dusk, saying that they would probably be seen but could not be caught before they were in the valley. Then the kidnappers would have to give up any search for them as hopeless. Carrie was all for reaching the road which must be somewhere at the top of the lane which led to the Abbey. She had not been brought up in the country and did not appreciate how easy it was to disappear into cover. A road, she insisted, meant cars and people and safety.

'If there are any cars so early,' Mike said doubtfully. 'But I suppose somebody is sure to pass, and anyone will do.'

On the other side of rising ground they found the road. Immediately below them was a slope of rough pasture running down to it which, further on, gave way to gorse bushes, the isolated clumps growing closer and closer until they formed solid thickets. The Abbey and the lane were out of sight. The road, bordered by low stone walls, remained empty, its surface blue and silent in the early light. Nothing was beyond it but peaceful fields, empty except for sheep.

They settled down in a green hollow so near the road that they had time to stop any traffic appearing from either direction. There they ate ravenously and drank the milk, finishing up with wild strawberries which hid, pink and white, among the tufts of grass. Mike recovered and felt ready for anything, though the sun had not yet risen above the sombre dawn clouds to the east and he was still cold.

'They will all have cleared off,' Carrie said. 'I might have escaped long ago and the police might be on the way.'

Mike did not think so and was sure they would have

a shot at finding her before they packed up and ran.

'Beard is the warden of the Abbey and knows the place. When he hears about the pigeons he'll guess that it was you who startled them. So you can't be far away yet.'

But Carrie was impatient. She went to stand by the roadside while Mike remained in the hollow eating strawberries. At last a car came along, travelling so fast that he had only time to get to his feet. The driver ignored Carrie's frantic waving. The filthy poncho, cut from a blanket, floated behind her. Her hair was wild and covered with dust from mortar and rotten wood. He may have thought that she was a gipsy running down to try and sell him something.

While she was still on the verge gazing after the vanished car, a man appeared at a curve higher up and started running towards her. A second later Beard vaulted a gate lower down the road and blocked her escape. Carrie scrambled back over the wall and dashed towards the gorse bushes with both men in hot pursuit.

Mike saw it all but was helpless. Carrie and her road! The minds of the kidnappers had worked on the same lines as hers. They had realised that they had only missed her by minutes and guessed that she would have run up to the road to try and attract somebody's attention. So Beard had charged right round the ruins and Screw had raced up the lane. If they failed to catch her between them or if they saw her picked up by a car they would know the worst immediately.

Instinctively Mike had dropped flat. Beard could not

possibly have seen him. Screw might have spotted his head when he was standing up, but was intent on Carrie and had shown no sign of noticing him. Looking out over the rim of the hollow he saw Carrie plunge into the thicket of gorse and watched her head twisting between the bushes until it disappeared.

His first impulse was to run straight down the road in the hope of coming to some house. But what might happen to Carrie meanwhile? Since the kidnappers did not know he was alive, Beard might think it was safe to return to his original plan and get rid of her down the well. By the time rescuers arrived it would be too late.

Should he show himself before bolting off for help? Wouldn't they then call off the chase and get away while the going was good? Possibly – but he had no time to sit down and think coldly about alternatives. He was terrified of leaving Carrie alone in the hands of such brutes. They were outside all his experience of human beings and he could put no limits to what they might or might not do. So the only certainty in his mind was that Carrie needed help and that he himself knew more about gorse brakes than any of them. He could stay close on their heels without them ever suspecting that he was in the thicket.

Carrie had entered that miniature, dark green forest at a point well marked by a late cluster of golden flowers. Beard and Screw were there now, pushing through or trampling down the spiny shoots; their tempers would not be improved by the prickles by the time they grabbed her or trod on her. Mike could guess what she had done when she vanished into the solidest part of the brake. She had come across an overgrown runway made by sheep or rabbits and bolted into it. That would not hold up her pursuers for long, especially since she could only get out very slowly at the other end, if at all.

Mike reached the lower end of the thicket by crouching down under cover of the roadside wall. There the bushes were sparse but just the right height. Running up the short turf between them he was perfectly protected and by standing on tiptoe he could see without being seen. The two men were above him and to his left, slowly and painfully beating out the patch where Carrie ought to be. Beard was now carrying her poncho which she must have slipped off when it caught in the gorse; wrapped around his forearm he found it useful for fending off branches. Mike could imagine her still and silent as any squatting rabbit and just as panic-stricken by the feet which crashed nearer and nearer.

He moved up along the little green rivers of turf until he was above her thicket of refuge and on the edge of a much larger one. She could not possibly have reached it unseen, but the two men, he decided, would not be as sure of that as he was. So he wormed his way into the gorse and made as much commotion as a startled ewe trying to get out. The two searchers were on to it at once, cursing Carrie and warning her that if she didn't come out they would tread her into the ground.

Mike silently left them to beat out the new thicket he had chosen for them and slipped away to the side where Carrie had entered the brake. He was growing more confident every minute and doubted if Beard and Screw would ever discover his existence. A dog would have had him at once, but to men – provided he was careful – he was elusive as an elf. Looking through the thin upper shoots he could see them from the waist up whenever he liked but they couldn't see him. It was seldom that he even had to bend down.

In the open, outside the thicket, he had to risk being seen. However, the men were still fully occupied and he had no trouble in reaching the yellow blossom where Carrie had dashed into cover. He twisted along the narrow ribbon of turf which she must have followed and found a strip of her poncho hanging on the spikes. This side of the patch was all trampled down and he could not be sure where was the little track or tunnel in which she had hidden. If he went any further, the tops of the bushes would begin to sway and might attract attention, so he risked calling to her quietly. Beard was damning and blasting away fifty yards uphill.

'Carrie! Carrie! Come towards me if you can! It's safe.'

They must have been within feet of her when they stopped searching, for she emerged at once, cracking dead stems and making far too much noise.

Beard heard it and shouted: 'There she is!' giving them just time to sneak down across open ground and re-enter the thicket. She followed Mike as he zig-zagged silently between bushes wherever there was a passage. When he stopped they had put a useful distance between themselves and the two hunters and had reached the far side of the brake where the gorse was more open but high enough to allow hide-and-seek – though a very risky hide-and-seek.

Now that they were together, the right game was to wait and see what Beard would do. There was also Chauffeur to be considered. Beard at one point had broken off the search in order to trot up to higher ground and wave to someone on the slopes below.

'If we could get back to the ruins while they are still looking for us here, there might be some visitors,' Carrie said.

'Not yet. I read a notice saying that it opens at ten. So I reckon there's about two and a half hours to go. And probably no one will turn up till much later.'

'Do you think there's a telephone there?'

'Did you see one when you were in the cottage?' he asked.

'No. But I wasn't looking.'

'There's a line running up the lane. Electricity, I expect.'

'They haven't got electricity. There was an oil stove in the kitchen.'

'And oil lamps!' he exclaimed. 'I remember seeing one through the window. There must be a telephone.'

'Then come on!'

The problem was how to get back to the Abbey. Whether they took to the road or ran over the open grass, Beard and Screw were bound to see them.

'We'll have to separate,' Mike said. 'I'll lead them a dance here so that you can reach the wall along the road. Keep your head well down and they won't see you! When you reach the lane run for the cottage! With luck you might meet another car on the way. If you're in any danger of being caught, get into the wood where the tents are!'

He pointed out the lowest clump of gorse, nearly on the edge of the road, and told her to run for it when he gave the word.

'And when you are safely behind it, watch through the branches! From where they are, they might catch sight of you on the far side of the wall, so I'll have to move them. As soon as you see that I'm keeping them busy, over you go and off to the telephone!'

It was difficult to know exactly what their two hunters were doing until their heads were seen threading through the gorse to tackle Carrie's original hiding place from the other side. When their backs were turned, she flitted across to the outlying clump and disappeared. She saw Mike darting from bush to bush and guessed that he was about to lead Beard up to the far corner of the gorse brake.

The move again worked like magic. They couldn't get at him – or her, as they thought – across the middle, so they ran round the top and plunged down for the thick patch where branches were swaying and crackling. She hoped that Mike had left himself a way of retreat. He seemed a little too sure of his woodland skill. But there was no time to watch. She had been told to jump into the road when she saw her chance, and this was it.

She crouched low and hurried as fast as bent knees would take her until she was round the curve of the road and out of sight of the gorse brake. The ruins and the lane leading to them were now in full view. There were no cars in the car park and not a soul to be seen among the grey-gold, crumbling ruins of the Abbey.

6

The Chase

Alone again without Mike, Carrie felt her determination oozing away. Since her dash into the gorse everything had gone so fast that it flicked through memory as if she had been a hunted animal with little, racing paws and no other thought. Now she had time to be afraid. The ruins were so bare and the hillside so exposed, with none of that cover where Mike was so confident. She felt that wherever she went there must be eyes looking at her and expressionless faces laughing at her. Her idea of reaching the telephone did not seem so bright any longer. It was surely better to run anywhere, and run and run rather than to show herself on the open lane and car park and to risk being caught and carried down again into that terrifying darkness.

It was the sun which made her go on. She loved the sun. Mike seemed to be at home whatever nature was up to, but for her – well, unless there was blue sky, indoors was as good as out. The sun rose clear of the dawn clouds and impulsively she lifted her arms to it in welcome. It made her misery appear as something which could never happen again. There was nothing to be afraid of, she told herself. Every police station in England must have been warned to look out for Carrie Falconer. She had only to lift the telephone and say that she was at Hilcote Abbey with Mike Prowse.

She ran down the lane and into the cottage. On her earlier visit she had found the kitchen wide open, had ransacked the larder and gone no further. Now she went straight past it into the living-room. No telephone there. A door led into the warden's office. She saw a counter, a hatch over it for selling tickets to visitors, some racks of handbooks and postcards and at last the telephone. There was no time for looking in the directory to find out if in that unknown district the police number was 999. She dialled the operator but heard no clicks. The telephone was dead.

She glanced round the room to see where the wires went. Perhaps there was a plug, and the kidnappers had merely disconnected it. But the wire ran up to the corner of the room and out with no break. She looked cautiously out of the front door. The wire crossed to the nearest pole all right, but where it emerged from the wall it had been cut. They had taken that precaution before they made their dash for the road which had so nearly caught her.

Now what? Mike had said that Chauffeur ought to be somewhere below the Abbey ready to intercept her if she showed herself on the long slope down to the valley. He might be still there or he might have joined the others at the gorse brake from which all that open country could be watched. The only safe route to people was to run back up the lane, turn right and keep running.

It was then that Chauffeur appeared. He was coming from the wood carrying two large packs which must be the tents and camping equipment all ready for instant departure. In another minute he would be at the cottage. There was no possible escape, for he could see both the living-room window and the front door. She jumped into the office in panic with a vague idea of locking the door against him. Then the ticket hatch caught her eye; it opened on the only side of the cottage which was out of his sight.

Carrie slid back the glass. Shoulders easily went through. With a kick and a wriggle she was upside down on the gravel walk outside. She picked herself up and was still on one knee when she heard Chauffeur enter the cottage and close the door. If he did not come into the office or go upstairs she was momentarily safe. She dashed across the path and a strip of lawn, then through an archway into a great square of crumbling walls, broken pillars and cobbles underfoot.

A notice read: THE CLOISTERS. Within the square she was hidden from the cottage but from nothing else. She ran round two sides, keeping close to the wall and looking through every arch for a hiding place. Notices pointed to THE REFECTORY, THE ABBOT'S KITCHEN, THE LIBRARY, but nothing was left of any of them beyond foundations enclosing carefully mown lawns. There wasn't a hiding place for a mouse.

Through still another arch she saw a pile of stone and earth and a notice: EXCAVATIONS, PLEASE KEEP OUT.

'And please jump in!' she said to herself.

At the brink of a long trench she hesitated, for the bottom was mud. Then she laughed at herself, remembering that mud would not make much difference to her appearance, jumped in and lay flat. Provided nobody had seen her, she counted on being safe until the kidnappers stopped looking for her and lit out for their usual haunts. With any luck a party of excavators might come along before then. Did nobody ever get out and about in this desolate country? She forgot that even on a school day she would only just be getting up.

After a few minutes getting her breath back in the mud, she was more self-possessed and saw no reason why she should not watch what, if anything, was happening. The excavators had cleared a stone trough, which lay on the edge of the trench, broken in half. Through the split she had a view of the cottage and the car park, and into the great square of the cloisters by way of an arch. Unless someone walked round the excavations she was safe.

Chauffeur dropped the packs outside the cottage. He strolled casually round the ruins, seeming quite at ease, and then chose a seat on the lawn of the Abbot's Kitchen. There he was quite close to Carrie. She had not seen him since he had driven up to her school. He looked just as a manservant ought to look – palish with a good, round stomach and solidly respectable. Anybody would trust him on sight.

In a few more minutes Screw came walking fast down the lane. Chauffeur, still preserving his air of calm, did not get up to meet him but beckoned him over.

'Any luck?' he asked.

'That boy's alive! We've got him.'

'How the hell's he alive?'

'Got out at the bottom of the well, so he tells us.'

'And the Falconer girl?'

'He says she came here to telephone.'

'Then we're for it! Grab those packs and get out!' Chauffeur yelled, losing all his dignified calm.

'It's O.K. I had cut the wire.'

'Thank God for that!'

'When was she here?' Screw asked.

'It must have been while I was packing up.'

'You didn't see her?'

'No. But she was in the office. The ticket window was open. I'll bet she nipped out of it while I was coming in at the door.'

'She's had time to get away?'

'Not up the lane and not into the wood. So she must be somewhere in the ruins.'

'Have you looked for her?'

'Not me! She'd be faster than I am. I just sat here to give the little lady confidence and let her bide till you two came back.'

It was the man's quiet manner which frightened Carrie even more than his accurate guess. He was so positive that she could not escape. And Mike! It did not sound as if they had murdered him on the spot. But how had they caught him and what had they done with him?

That was soon answered. Beard came trotting across the fields with a bundle under his arm rolled up in the poncho. The bundle looked very still. When Beard came up to his companions she was relieved that two legs were sticking out and kicking; but they were tied together so that the movements were helpless as those of a beetle on its back.

The three had a quick talk too far away for her to overhear it. Then Chauffeur, who had said he was no runner, remained with Mike in the cottage. Beard and Screw, who most certainly could run, started to search the ruins, passing round the outside of the cloisters. Carrie lay still at the bottom of her trench, hoping in vain that she could not be distinguished from earth.

'Come out of there, sweetie! We don't want to get our shoes muddy.'

She dashed out of the trench on the opposite side, but Beard jumped it easily, grabbed her by the hair and simultaneously put a hand over her mouth. He carried her into the cottage and quickly gagged her with an old sock, taping it in place.

All three men were now in the room with them. Mike was unbundled and efficiently gagged before he had a chance to speak. He exchanged a miserable glance with Carrie and they looked away from each other. So far as she could see, he was unhurt. Beard said coolly that they all deserved some breakfast and went to the larder. He came back with three bottles of beer, only remarking that the little blighters must have pinched the bread and the ham. Carrie expected to get at least a kick in the ribs as he passed but he paid no attention to her. That frightened her more than if he had sworn at her. All three ignored them. They didn't exist any more once they were caught.

The distant noise of a car coming down the lane was unmistakable. Mike and Carrie stared at each other, round eyes sparkling with hope. Someone was coming, would break in, would find them.

'There's a car!' Screw exclaimed, and threw open the window at the back of the house ready to jump through it.

'Shut that!' Beard ordered sharply, and went on in a gentle voice, 'No hurry. Nobody knows a thing.

Whoever they are, I'll let 'em walk round. One never knows. They might be useful witnesses if there's ever any trouble. You keep these two quiet!'

The car stopped outside. Beard went into the office and slid back the ticket window. They heard him say:

'I'm sorry. We're not open yet . . . Oh well, if it's your only chance to see the Abbey . . . Two? Forty pence, please . . . Yes, founded in 1146, dissolved by Henry VIII in 1539 . . . Yes, extraordinary how little is left, isn't it? But when one remembers that everything of value was carted away and that then people came from miles around to pull down stone and timber for building it is not surprising that the rest collapsed. After that the Abbey just vanished under weeds and woodland. Very wild country up here! Big sheep runs, and that's all. So nobody cared until sixty years ago Lord Hilcote bought the estate and took his title from it. He had the ruins cleared and opened to the public . . . Yes, certainly I will walk round with you if you like. I've nothing else to do so early.'

Beard closed the ticket window and went out through the front door. They heard his voice lecturing away as footsteps crunched on gravel and disappeared.

'Cor! He's got a nerve!' Chauffeur said.

'Comes easy! He does it every day.'

'I don't know how he finds time for other business.'

'The Abbey's closed in winter.'

'What else has he used it for – I mean, down there?'

'Art robberies. Anything else that needs keeping on ice,' Screw said. 'And there was the French boy. When he was returned to his dear parents, he couldn't tell 'em a thing. Never knew he had left France!'

'A pity he can't sell this pair!' Chauffeur complained. 'We'll have to wait for the next job before we can retire.'

'He'll never let you.'

'Then the job has to be big enough. That's all I say!'

The unseen visitors returned. Beard kept them in conversation outside the open front door, even allowing them a view of the unoccupied end of the living-room.

A woman's voice said:

'What a wonderful thing religion was!'

'And is. Is still,' Beard replied reverently.

'My husband and I are so glad that the Abbey has somebody like you to look after it, and not a student or a little man in a peaked cap.'

'I am afraid they are all the Trust usually can afford, madam. But fortunately I have a small income of my own and can make myself useful where I see a need.'

The car drove off, and hardly had the hum of its engine died away when a motor-bike came roaring down the lane. Carrie's agonised disappointment again turned to hope. The place was waking up.

'God! The gardener!' Chauffeur muttered. 'The risks he runs!'

'There wouldn't be any if that boy hadn't got loose.'

The motor-bike stopped, started again, and the silence of the hills returned. Beard came in.

'I sent him down to the village to mow the church-yard,' he explained. 'That'll take him all the morning. Always glad to help the Vicar, we are!'

'You ought to have a car here,' Screw said.

'I never have a car where I live. It's just one more

84

thing that can be traced. Now it's time to take sweetie and her boy friend back to their home.'

'Got some more dope to give 'em a shot?'

'It will not be used. It's getting late and we'll take no chances. Do you want to be seen carrying two bodies from here to the wood? Put your packs on your backs and lead them over into the trees! No gags. No lashings. From a distance you will appear natural – two men and their children happily camping. If they start to utter a sound, you will make them wish they hadn't and prevent any more. Then come back here and leave the rest to me! I'm going over now to check up on the wood itself.'

In five minutes Beard returned from reconnoitring the path and reported that all was clear. Lashings on wrists and ankles were cut and gags removed; but Carrie and Mike were utterly helpless. Screw took her arm and Chauffeur took Mike's. From a distance, as Beard had said, the contact may have looked affection-ate; in fact each powerful arm was interlocked with a small one and a brutal grip kept on the wrist.

Carrie did not struggle. Mike tried to drag his feet in the hope of that unlikely person on the horizon notic-ing that this was no friendly walk with Dad. Chauffeur threatened to break his arm and gave him such agony for a moment that he waited for the crack. Neither of them dared to make a sound.

They came to the bank at the edge of the wood and the entrance to their prison. As they stood there, Carrie gave Mike a smile and half a wink in full view of Chauf-feur. It was unlike her, and Mike could not understand what she had to smile about. He assumed it was just bravado and did his best to smile back. Chauffeur looked from one to the other suspiciously. Carrie met his eyes with an angelic look of innocence.

They passed the children from one to another down the ladder. It seemed that Chauffeur had never entered the barn before. He held the lantern high above his head and said it all looked very dangerous.

Seeing the ruinous mess lit up for the first time, Mike agreed with him. No wonder they could not find their way at night! Unlike the cellar below with its solid arches and pillars, the barn was a shapeless maze of fallen beams, broken posts and roots, the hollows beneath them separated by mounds of earth and timber.

'It's all safe enough if we keep close to the wall,' Screw assured his companion. 'Those monks couldn't scamp the job in case the Abbot sacked 'em. Wonderful thing is religion, as the lady said. Come on! We have only to put them down.'

Screw lifted the grating and dragged Mike and Carrie to the bottom of the steps. Neither of them tried to resist. This was the end.

'I don't think we should leave them here alone,' Chauffeur said.

'Gawd! Going soft on us?'

'Not me! I use my loaf, that's all. I was just thinking that the boy escaped down the well.'

'Well, he won't any more. There's no way down and he'd break his neck.'

'The water may be too deep for that. Where is it?' Chauffeur asked.

'Through the arch there, in the far corner. What's

wrong with you? He told us just to shut them up and clear off.'

The two were about to leave them when Chauffeur uneasily returned to the subject.

'That girl – I caught her smiling at her little boy friend when she saw they were being put down again.'

'Maybe it's a home from home by this time.'

'It looked to me as if it was what they wanted.'

Screw hesitated. He acknowledged there might be something in that and said he didn't want to spend the rest of his young days in the nick.

'Well, you stay here while I run over and see the boss and tell him what you suspect,' he suggested.

He went up the stone stairs and put back the grating in passing. Chauffeur sat on the second step with the lantern.

Carrie broke down and started to cry pitifully.

'Let us go, mister,' she sobbed. 'You can't do this. It isn't fair. You're a kind man really. You know you are.'

She knelt at his feet, stroking his leg. Chauffeur was embarrassed.

'Now, now!' he said. 'Don't cry! Perhaps your Dad will pay up yet. Just you wait and see!'

With a sweep of the hand which had been stroking his leg Carrie knocked over the lantern and jumped on it.

'The well!' she snapped at Mike, grabbing his hand.

They could see almost nothing in the sudden darkness, but they knew without eyes the way to the second cellar and the well. As soon as they were through the archway, Carrie pulled him round the corner and both stood flat against the wall. Chauffeur felt his way after them, bumping into a pillar but very close behind. When he was past the arch and aiming for the well, Carrie tip-toed fast for the steps, Mike with her. He did not dare to speak for fear of being heard, but thought it useless to go back to the main cellar – the one place where there was a little light.

Carrie rushed up the steps and threw back the grating with a clang. Only then did he remember that he had never heard the bolt go home. She must have noticed it at the time.

Chauffeur could see them now. There was no chance even to think of shutting him in. They ran straight for the grey light of the entrance, jumping fallen beams while Chauffeur pounded after them, taking more care with his route through obstacles which he did not know and could barely see.

Carrie was up the ladder in a second. Mike, following her through the hole, felt a grab for his leg and kicked out with the other. A hardness at the heel of his boot and a yell of pain told him he had connected.

The wood was too open and unsafe. He knew that in the end they could be surrounded and caught there. He raced across the clearing where the tents had been, Carrie following his lead. Chauffeur was up the ladder and out. He heard him yelling to Beard and Screw. The only chance was to get clear of the trees before they came up.

Out in the open he swerved left in the opposite direction to the ruins, not working it out but obeying an instinct which told him that the pursuers would expect them either to hide in the wood or to run straight down hill across the bare fields for the unknown village.

A bunch of sheep, peacefully grazing, was in front of them. They lifted their heads, about to trot away. The gang could hardly miss the meaning of a flock of sheep charging off over the grass.

'Don't let them run! Don't let them run!' Mike prayed.

He dropped flat and signalled Carrie to do the same. The sheep watched them suspiciously but still did not run. Mike, now with shoulders raised, was behaving exactly like a sheep dog holding them steady. They moved off a little, looked back and continued to graze.

Very slowly he twisted his head to see what was happening. Screw was working his way through the sparse undergrowth at the edge of the wood. He did not stop to examine the open ground at all. Obviously he must have given it a casual glance – in the wrong direction – as soon as he arrived; but since the fugitives were not running for dear life they could not be there.

The obliging sheep, finding that they were not expected to do anything in particular and that the human dog had apparently gone to sleep, quietly moved further on. Where they had been was now revealed as a very slight fold of ground sprinkled with molehills of rich, red-brown earth, some trampled flat, some of overnight freshness. It occurred to Mike that the lump of Carrie's back, plastered with the drying mud of the trench, was much the same colour. If only they could reach the molehills unobserved, the dip might be just enough to protect them, lying flat, from eyes in or outside the wood. It gave no cover from anyone out in the open below the Abbey, but at that distance it would be hard to distinguish them from the work of moles.

He whispered to Carrie to crawl very slowly to the molehills and lie down.

'I'll be watching the wood,' he added. 'If there's danger I'll baa like a sheep. Then curl up and don't move! When I baa again you can go on.'

Carrie set off. He could tell from rustling movements in the trees that someone there was fully occupied – only one of them, for he heard no voices. Probably the other was up on the bank, covering the far side of the wood in case they tried to break out there and run for the road. He risked twisting round to look behind him. It was as well that he did. Beard had left the searching of the wood to his accomplices and was walking down from the direction of the Abbey at his usual fast but unhurried pace. He carried a twelve-bore gun under his arm.

'Baa! Baa!'

He did not dare to move his head back again and could only hope that Carrie had frozen.

Beard, half turned away, continued on over the open field.

'Baa!'

He thought his second bleat sounded high and frightened like that of a late lamb left behind by its mother; but Beard noticed nothing wrong with it and went steadily on as if quite sure of what he had planned.

It was now safe to turn round and watch the wood again. Nothing was going on there. He caught a glimpse of Chauffeur at the corner nearest to the Abbey. He was holding a handkerchief to his nose and his shirt was striped with red.

He looked for Carrie but she had mysteriously vanished. A second glance discovered between two molehills a third which had an unnaturally round top. However, if it had not at first been obvious to him that it was Carrie's bottom, it certainly wasn't going to be obvious to anyone else.

Beard for the moment was out of sight, so Mike wormed his way over to the dip and lay down full length where the sheep had scattered and trampled the earth of several molehills. That ought to provide reasonable camouflage if not examined too closely.

'Do you think we're safe?' Carrie whispered.

'Yes, for where they are now. But Beard is below us somewhere and might come up past us.'

'How did they catch you?'

'A lousy hare!'

He explained that he had lured them into a patch of gorse which they were beating out, convinced that Carrie was hiding there. Meanwhile he was kneeling on one knee, not far away from them, where the bushes were more open and he could slip silently from one to another. Right under his nose a hare burst out of cover.

'She was squatting down in her form as frightened as you had been,' he said. 'I could have touched her but I never saw her. Then her nerve broke and she galloped away. A big old lady she was, and she made a thud and a crackling which she'd never have done on grass. Beard was round my bush in a couple of jumps. By golly, he can move fast! I couldn't shake him off and that was that.'

Carrie told him how she, too, had been caught, that the telephone had been cut and that visitors to the

Abbey would be no help unless they could reach them before Beard.

'And that's not likely,' Mike said. 'Our only chance is to try for the hanger with the spring in it. They'll never let us reach the ruins or the road. They *have* to get us. If they don't they'll be in for kidnapping and attempted murder. Oh, Carrie, you were so brave!'

'Me? When?'

'When we thought it was the end and you smiled at me.'

'Oh, that! Chauffeur was losing his cool. Didn't you notice?'

'No, I did not. I was wondering if there was any way to get out by the well-head.'

'I did notice. So I thought I'd try to fool him and then perhaps he would do something silly. That was why I smiled and winked at you – to make him think twice before shutting us up again. And then – well, the lantern was so close and I can always cry if it's going to do me any good.'

'I wish I paid more attention to people. You're brilliant,' Mike said.

'And I wish I paid more to molehills. I think we're rather good together, Mike.'

'Keep your fingers crossed! What do you suppose they will do now?'

'Well, they must be sure that we aren't in the wood. And we haven't gone for the road and we aren't in the open. I know! We must have gone back underground.'

'If you're right, Screw is searching that now.'

'How do you know?'

'Chauffeur is between the wood and the cottage, and

Beard has gone to look for us lower down. He has a shot-gun with him now. I didn't tell you.'

'Is he allowed to carry one, Mike?'

'Why not? He's probably got the right to pot rabbits round the Abbey.'

'I'd stop if he shot at me.'

'Well, I wouldn't and nor will you. Remember that if it's more than fifty yards he is only going to pepper your bottom. You might have to eat your breakfast standing up for a day or two.'

'How far is fifty yards?'

'About half the distance to the edge of the wood.'

'Do you think Beard can see us?'

Mike cautiously wriggled round. Below them was the long, dry-stone wall dividing the slope. They could never have reached it, but Beard evidently thought it possible that they had. His head was visible bobbing along behind it.

'Yes, he could see us if we didn't look like molehills. But I don't think he can see the ground at the edge of the wood.'

'Go on then! Try and reach it and run for the road while Screw is underground!'

It was the last thing Mike wanted to try. Carrie had far too much faith in his gift for moving unseen. But this was almost a dare. And it was true that if he could reach the top of the lane, he was bound to meet somebody before long.

'All right! But, Carrie, you must promise to stay here and not move an inch.'

He set off, wishing to heaven that he really was a mole. At first it was Beard he was afraid of. He could only trust that the brute was occupied in poking about in thistles and bramble at the foot of the wall. Once out of the dip and on the flat, where he was above Beard's line of sight, he lay still, panting with relief.

Now Screw was the danger. Carrie had been simply guessing when she exclaimed that he would be underground. It was more likely that Screw would loose off a shout of triumph and come charging out of the wood towards him before he could get to his feet. Then Beard would race up past Carrie and couldn't miss her.

He must go faster, faster! But faster he could not without getting to his feet. He did the last bit scurrying on hands and knees. The wood remained quite silent. He entered the undergrowth and stood up.

Moving from tree to tree, he crossed the path through the wood and caught a glimpse of Chauffeur guarding the way to the Abbey. Screw was up on the bank with a full view over the fields to the road. So Carrie's plan was hopeless. But she had been partly right. Screw must have made a quick search underground, for the ladder had been pulled up, ensuring that if they were hiding down there after all and he had missed them they could not get out.

Mike returned to the undergrowth at the edge of the trees to see what Beard was up to now. After searching the length of the wall until satisfied that the children could never have got so far unseen, he was coming back, continually making sudden changes of direction like a hound following a scent.

His plan was easily understood by Mike, who had often been out with his great-uncle to watch shoots over the big estate where he had been gamekeeper, and himself had earned some pocket money as a beater. Chauffeur and Screw were like the guns at the edge of a covert, and Beard was going to drive the game towards them, wherever the hell it was. For the moment he was safe enough, but Beard was bound to spot that Carrie was not a molehill.

There was no way to help her. He realised with horror that there was nothing he could do. Carrie lying down was out of sight, so he could not signal her to run. And if she did run it would be for the wood, which was just what Beard wanted.

Beard abruptly changed direction again, this time heading for the Abbey and walking fast. It was essential to know what had disturbed him, and Mike risked a short sprint along the turf of the path before popping back into cover. Chauffeur was where he ought to be, blocking the way to the ruins and waving to his boss to come up. Mike approached as closely as he dared without leaving the trees and soon saw the reason. Three bicycles were leaning up against the notice board. They must have free-wheeled silently down the lane while he was watching Beard.

Finding nobody to sell them a ticket, the cyclists were strolling round the Abbey. He caught a glimpse of them on the far side of the cloisters. Three hearty young men they were, busily taking notes. He thought of yelling, 'Help! I am Mike Prowse!' but they had passed beyond the cloisters to the excavations, where they might hear a shout but not what he said. Screw had moved closer; Chauffeur and Beard were only a stone's throw away. They would have him down in the dark again before the cyclists came along to investigate, if they ever did. So it was best to wait for them to return to the cycles.

That soon became impossible. He heard Chauffeur say:

'Right, boss! Through the wood again and look up into every tree!'

Beard remained where he was, watching from a safe distance every move of the cyclists. From his point of view it was just conceivable that Mike and Carrie might be found by them in the ruins and, if they were, he wanted to be the first to know. Meanwhile Screw and Chauffeur were about to enter the wood. Mike slipped away in front of them and dashed across the open to drop into position alongside Carrie.

He whispered quickly what had happened and that Beard would soon be back to continue his search.

'Not soon. Not till the cyclists have gone,' she said. 'He must be afraid – so very afraid – that we can reach them somehow. Beard won't take his eyes off them till they have ridden away.'

'Then we'll try and get behind the wall down there. He's already searched it. When they spot us, keep running for the hanger in the valley! It's a rotten chance, Carrie, but I think it's our only one.'

'It's a jolly good one,' she replied. 'Remember that if either of us gets clear they daren't do anything much to the other!'

Mike did not feel at all sure of that, considering all the anger they must be feeling. He crawled a few yards until he could look out of the dip. Beard was still watching the cyclists. Chauffeur and Screw could be heard plunging about in the wood and certainly were not anywhere near the edge of it.

'Run, Carrie!'

They reached the dry-stone wall, scrambled over and dropped behind it. They had not been seen, but they had startled the sheep. Beard at once showed up on the slope below the ruins and a moment later Screw dashed out of the trees. They did not immediately aim for the wall, assuming that the children had started from the ground where the sheep had been and were trying to run right round the wood.

'Run!' Mike snapped again.

As soon as they jumped up they were seen, but they had a useful lead which might be enough to take them into the hanger. All three were after them – Chauffeur the most dangerous since he only had to go straight down the hill to cut them off.

7

Mike Breaks Away

Over the short, sheep-cropped turf they went, racing down the hill to the hanger where Mike had emerged from the spring into daylight. Far off, rising above soft green waves of rich, well-timbered land, was the church tower which promised safety if once they could escape from these bleak uplands. Carrie tripped and fell, but Chauffeur could get no closer; he had lost ground while clumsily climbing over the wall. Screw had jumped a gap in his stride and was overhauling them fast. Beard with his usual cunning had left the direct chase and was going hard for the bottom end of the hanger to stop the way out of it.

Chauffeur, now plugging along, swung right for the top, leaving it to Screw to run down the pair. Mike began to tire and to trail behind Carrie whose legs twinkled down the hill. She reached the cover first and vanished into the hazels. Remembering that it was enough if only one of them could escape, Mike swerved away and gave Screw the choice of which he would catch. He chose Carrie, determined not to let her out of his sight, for he must have been exasperated by the continual nuisance she had made of herself.

Mike now had a few seconds to find a refuge, for he could go no further. Though his pursuers had been warned to look up into trees, he had to take one. It was

the only possible place. Thick boa constrictors of old
ivy were strangling a dying ash; falling strands and a
dead branch offered a way up. He wriggled into a fork
and clung there panting. At least he would be invisible
to anyone directly underneath. Neither the dead branch
nor the ivy would support the weight of a grown man,
which was so much to the good. On the other hand it
would be very simple for Beard to blast a shot into the
curtain of green on the off-chance that he was there.

He could not see where on earth Carrie had got to.
Screw from time to time was in view, beating out the
hazels. The perpetual, snarling smile was off his face at
last. He, too, was exhausted and stopped for a moment
with his hand on a tree to get his breath back. It was
lucky that he had never come to a standstill earlier or
he would have heard Mike.

Carrie seemed to have learned quickly from experience. The moss under her light feet would have helped
quiet movement, but she was the wrong colour now –
brownish when she should have been green. Could she
have escaped? He thought it unlikely, for the hazels
were well spaced and the hanger more open than the
Abbey wood. She had not a long enough lead.

He saw the vixen and her two cubs slip out of the
depression where her earth was and noticed how
cleverly she did it, not caring how close she passed
Screw so long as he was upwind and weeds were high
enough to cover the family. Nearly under his tree they
froze and he could see the vixen's muzzle twitching.
They slipped back into cover and broke out lower
down, loping leisurely off across the open and shining
red and white in the sun.

99

He looked for the reason why she had changed her mind, and then saw Carrie – or rather her two feet. She was in an appallingly dangerous position, not far from Screw and not in cover at all. What she had done was to twist back on her tracks into the open again. She was lying outside the hanger, hidden from Screw by a low, thin straggle of bramble and not hidden at all if he left the trees. Beard was a still worse threat; he had only to walk up over the turf and he would not have to chase Carrie any more. He could deal with the body after dark.

Screw shouted that he had lost them. Beard from somewhere down below shouted back that he should work uphill, crossing and recrossing the copse. They were trapped again, and the chance of anyone coming along was even less likely than at the Abbey. Chauffeur was ready for them at the top of the hanger. At the bottom was Beard with his gun. The three could spend the day there if necessary and leave the ruins to look after themselves.

Screw moved off. Mike dropped to the ground and hissed to Carrie to join him quickly.

'I knew you were there,' she said. 'I saw you.'

'How did you fool him?'

'I dodged round the trunk of that big beech. I could nearly have touched him as he passed. And then I crawled.'

'I know where to put you if we can reach it. We'll have a few minutes before Screw reaches the top and comes back.'

He led the way to the fox's earth, slinking over the mossy floor into the middle of the hanger. Close around the earth weeds and stunted elders were mixed with the hazel, all looking untidy and twisted, with dead roots trailing on the surface. The entrance was on the bank of a hollow – the only part of the hanger where the slope was not even – and below it was scattered raw, fine soil, more yellow there than red.

'Phew! It pongs!' Carrie whispered.

'Never mind that! Some people like it. Get in feet first and go down as far as you can!'

'Are you coming in too?'

'No. I'll get clear – or make them think I have, which comes to the same thing. Now I'm going to cover you up.'

At some time in the winter the earth had been blocked by the hunt to prevent a fox taking refuge in it. Old hawthorn and bits of wood were lying close by.

'Wait! I've got an idea!' she exclaimed. 'Take my shoes and – oh, anything! – my hair ribbon! Put them by the spring you came out of! They'll think we are inside.'

It was brilliant. Beard could not know it was impossible to force a way in through the spring. Mike had only said that he got out that way, without details.

She squirmed up and passed out the shoes and hair ribbon. Mike quickly stopped the earth well enough to hide her, leaving most of the hunt's debris where it was. It was unlikely that Screw on his return would look too closely at the patch of bare, broken ground all over again.

He was coming back now. Mike smoothed the soil so that no tracks remained and slipped away ahead of him just in time. He crept down the hanger to find out what Beard was doing and found him out in the open patrolling the bottom. That was all right. Evidently he meant to wait there until the fugitives dashed out or Screw joined him. Mike then visited the spring pool and left Carrie's shoes at the edge of the water as if they had been carelessly kicked off and forgotten – just like a fleeing, frightened girl, Beard would think, but not in the least like the real Carrie. Her hair ribbon he wound into the rushes at the outlet of the pool, apparently washed there by the water.

The best plan now was to lie up as near to the open as he could get and wait for a chance to escape. Anything might happen, but there was a fair chance that Beard would go rushing up to the spring without searching on the way as soon as Screw made the discovery.

The most tempting cover was in the stream under a wild rose bush which arched over it. Mike did not like it. For one thing he had had quite enough of icy water; for another it might occur to Screw or Beard to look for more clues downstream. The only alternative was a fallen fir, half of which lay in the open. That would have to do, provided he could crawl there while Beard's back was turned.

It was the sort of risk he would never have dreamed of taking if he had not got used to risks during the hours since dawn. As it was, he did not even crawl but made four quick, silent steps and dropped to the ground alongside the tree trunk and half under it. He heard Screw coming nearer. The man was doing a more thorough job than when he had made a snap search of the hazels, sure he would find Carrie. On each journey

across the hanger he went right outside before return-
ing. Mike squeezed himself still further under the log.
He had reckoned on being fairly safe from Beard, but
Screw might well take more than a casual glance.

All was silent. Mike hoped that Screw had arrived at
the pool and was examining it with special curiosity.

'Boss! Here! Take a look at this!'

Beard charged into the hazels.

'I don't believe it's possible,' Mike heard him say.

'Well, he told you he had come out there, and he
couldn't have broken out of the well any other way.
He can't fly!'

Beard splashed through the pool.

'Here's a vent big enough for a child's body,' he said
doubtfully, 'but the water is coming up through gravel.
Hey, and this one! This is it! The boy's footmarks and
turf torn away. Solid rock it looks on both sides. You
and I wouldn't have a hope, but they could get in if
they didn't drown doing it.'

There was more splashing. They had found the hair
ribbon now.

'So that's the end of our troubles!' Beard exclaimed
with relief. 'Lucky for us she forgot to take her shoes
with her! Now you two can go back and clean up all
trace of them. I'll stay here above the spring all day and
all night if I must. I can see them as soon as they come
out and they can't see me. They never will see me if it
comes to that.'

Mike gave Screw and Chauffeur time to reach the
Abbey. Then he crawled out and reconnoitred the pool.
Beard was where he said he would be – sitting on the
slab of rock above the spring where Mike had warmed

himself back to life the day before. He was smoking a cigarette with his gun by his side. The range to those two heads which he expected to appear was not more than ten yards.

Satisfied that Beard could not see beyond the surrounding hazels, Mike slipped out of the hanger and trotted down to that longed-for, peaceful valley and the village which must be under the church tower.

He felt like Rip Van Winkle appearing after a hundred years. The world was going on as usual. It surprised him. Two women, gaily chattering, came out of the butcher's. There were a pram and a dog outside the village shop. At the gate of an empty cottage a builder was taking ladders off his van. A man stood talking to another who was cutting the privet hedge in front of his garden. The church clock said quarter to eleven.

All this was unreal as a photograph. He realised that everyone was standing still and staring at the ragged, filthy boy running down the middle of the street. He chose the man talking over the hedge, who looked fatherly and responsible.

'Is there a police station here?' he asked.

'Not any more. But we can usually call up one of their cars within ten minutes. What's the trouble, son?'

'I'm Mike Prowse. Have you heard of me?'

'Heard of you! Look at that!'

He pointed to a placard outside 'J. G. Midwinter, Newsagent and Tobacconist'. It read:

NO NEWS OF MISSING CHILDREN
POLICE BAFFLED

He ran into the shop with Mike, saying that he was

Midwinter and had just stepped out for a breath of air. He grabbed the telephone on the counter.

'Police? Listen, I've got Mike Prowse here . . . No, I'm not the kidnapper . . . He's just walked into Hilcote . . . Damn my name and address! . . . Get a car here quick! He looks as if he'd been buried alive . . . Yes, Hilcote and I'm J. G. Midwinter . . . Hold on and I'll ask him! Any news of Carrie Falconer, Mike?'

'She's all right but in danger.'

Mr Midwinter repeated it, and told the police to leave that cup of tea and hurry.

'Can I call my parents?' Mike asked.

'Go right ahead!'

Mike dialled his home and at once heard his father's voice. Being always out and about he rarely answered the telephone, leaving it to Janet.

'Dad, this is Mike. I'm free.'

He thought he heard a gasp and a sob. Anyway there was something wrong with his father's voice, but he couldn't be crying because he never did.

'Where are you, dear?'

'A place called Hilcote.'

'Where's that?'

Mike had to ask his friend.

'It's in Warwickshire, close to the Gloucestershire border. On the Cotswolds.'

'Mum and I will be there in an hour and a bit.'

'Let the Falconers know that Carrie is in a safe place and was O.K. when I went for help!'

'Well, that's fine,' said Mr Midwinter. 'What would you like while we wait for the cops?'

'I'd like to go to sleep, but I mustn't. Can I have a bath?'

'No time for that either, son. Try a quick shower! And there may be some clothes around of your size that once belonged to our boy. The wife has gone into town, but I think I can find 'em. She can't bear to throw them away, you know. Hungry?'

'Very, Mr Midwinter.'

'I'll rustle up some breakfast while you change. No harm in talking to the police with your mouth full!'

The police car drew up outside Midwinter's shop while Mike was still on his first egg. A constable came in, pulled out a photograph, compared it with Mike and said it was not the right boy.

'You wouldn't look the same, copper, either if you'd been kept in the dark for four days and had to run for your bleeding life,' said Mr Midwinter, who had now heard part of Mike's story. 'He has just talked to his father.'

A second car arrived, this time with a uniformed Inspector and a detective sergeant in plain clothes. They sensibly let Mike run through his adventures without wasting time in questions until he came to Beard, when the Inspector exclaimed:

'What! Botswinger, the Warden! But he's never off the place except in winter.'

'He doesn't have to be when visitors can come and see him there,' the Sergeant said. 'Do you remember that Swiss crook, sir, whom we were asked to keep tabs on? He drove out to see the Abbey.'

'By Jove, so he did, Bill! And we thought nothing of it at the time.'

'You must get up to Carrie Falconer quick,' Mike interrupted, and told them where she was.

'I can take you right to that earth,' Mr Midwinter offered. 'Same vixen, they say, every summer year after year. It's my opinion that the hunt don't want to catch her.'

'We'd be very grateful, Mr Midwinter. Now, if the boy is right, Screw and Chauffeur, as he calls 'em, will be up at the Abbey at present. Once they get away they may take some finding. Will they be on their guard, Mike?'

'I shouldn't think so. They believe we are safely inside the spring. It's impossible really. But they don't know that.'

'Well, I shall want you to go with the Sergeant here to identify them in case they mix themselves up with a party of visitors. Feel up to it?'

Mike said there was nothing he'd like better than to see them both run in. The Inspector turned to his colleague and gave his orders.

'We'll pick them up first, Bill, so that they haven't a chance to warn Botswinger. You had better take two men with you. They may have learned a few disappearing acts from Mike here. When you have them, call me! My party will be in the valley and then move on the spring to catch him with his gun. I want that, if possible. It bears out the boy's story. You know what his counsel will say in court – just innocently looking for a rabbit and the boy was so frightened that he imagined the rest. Then he'll only get seven years instead of the fifteen we want for him. Any questions?'

'No, sir. That's quite clear. Tell my men to meet me at Gallows Hill Crossroads! Tourists they'll be. Plain car and plain clothes.'

The Inspector picked up the telephone and began to talk to police headquarters. After thanking Mr Midwinter – who forced on him a bar of chocolate the size of a book, saying that he hadn't had time to finish his breakfast – Mike got into the car with the Sergeant and raced out of the village.

They waited at Gallows Hill Crossroads until two men turned up in a plain grey car. The Sergeant introduced them as Constable Peters and Constable Ridgway, but never called them anything but Sam and George. Mike could hardly believe that they were detectives. One wore a beret on his long, fair hair and looked rather like a foreign student; the other was slung with cameras, one of which was a cleverly disguised walkie-talkie. That explained something which had puzzled Mike – how the Sergeant could call the Inspector when neither was near a telephone.

The Sergeant left his police car to be picked up later, and together with Mike joined Sam and George. They took the road above the Abbey. The gorse brake shone dark green under the midday sun, looking as if nothing more deadly than picking wild strawberries could ever have happened there. Mike shivered and said that was where Beard caught him.

'He didn't hurt you?'

'Not much. He hadn't any time to waste. He thought at first that Carrie had been able to telephone.'

'After the dance you had led him I wonder he didn't drag you through a gorse bush,' the Sergeant said. 'Where did you learn it all?'

'From my Great-uncle Jim. The best gamekeeper in the county, he was. He can put his cap on a stick and walk round and round a hare until he picks her out of her form by the ears.'

'Blimey! Good shot too?'

'Now that he's old he does sometimes miss, Sergeant.'

They coasted in neutral down the lane to the Abbey and stopped in the car park. No other vehicle was there. The Sergeant got out and rattled the ticket window as if he were a tourist anxious to pay his fee and get on with it. Sam, outside the front door of the cottage, innocently admired the scenery. George was on the nearest of the Abbey lawns, from which he could cover the bit of garden and the living-room window.

Finding no response to his rattling, the Sergeant entered the cottage. Nobody was at home. Returning to the car where Mike was curled up out of sight on the floor, he asked:

'What do you think? You know how their minds work.'

'I don't,' Mike answered. 'You need Carrie for that. I just sometimes know where they won't look for me, and that's different.'

'It seems much the same to me.'

It was not at all the same, but Mike ventured a guess:

'Well, Beard told them to clear up. They might have left it till now and be down below.'

'Show us the way in then!'

'Of course, you know best, but if they aren't there they might see you before you see them and run,' Mike suggested very politely. 'I can't spot their packs, so they could be setting up their tents again now that they think they are safe. Shall I go first and tell you where they are?'

'You? You've had enough, son.'

'You see, I know every inch of that wood by now, Sergeant.'

'Something in that! It would save trouble to grab 'em before they have any suspicions. But don't you be seen or heard and come straight back!'

Mike reached the edge of the clearing without any trouble. It was a relief to be hunting instead of the hunted. Screw and Chauffeur were there. Their tents were up. Screw was pumping up a paraffin stove which was just beginning to burn. Chauffeur lay lazily on his back with a rolled sleeping-bag under his head. Mike recognised it as Carrie's bag, for it had a rip where she had scratched it open with her nails while crazy with loneliness before he had been dragged in to join her. So in fact they had cleared up the cellar, and it was as well that the police had not gone directly to it and given themselves away.

He was amazed how guiltless they looked, that pair of fellows enjoying the sunshine and open air. They could be taken for schoolmasters interested in abbeys, or excavators, or plain campers who had found the same peace as in the time of the monks and decided to stay a night or two.

He slid out of the wood again and returned to the police with his report.

'Sam, you go round the wood well out in the open and take position on the far side!' the Sergeant ordered. 'We shall go straight up the path. And you stay here, son!'

He gave Sam plenty of time to get round the wood and then set off with George. When they were out of sight, Mike disobeyed orders. By this time he had as strong a dislike of open car parks as any wild animal. Besides, Beard might want a drink or more cigarettes and leave the spring to come up to the cottage. The wood was the only place where he felt reasonably safe until all three were arrested. He drifted into it and up towards the clearing to see what happened.

As the police approached up the path, Screw and Chauffeur did not even get up but lazily wished them good morning.

'Been looking at the Abbey?'

'Not yet,' the Sergeant answered. 'We want somebody to show us round.'

'The Warden is away. Just walk round by yourselves! Have you come by car?'

'We did.'

'That's funny. I didn't hear you.'

'You're hiking yourselves?'

'Yes. That's the way to see country!'

It was amazing how sure they were that they could not be suspected. Mike, expecting to see an immediate arrest with perhaps a bit of a punch-up before handcuffs were snapped on the criminals, thought that the police were in doubt and did not realise that they were just about to jump the pair before they could suspect anything.

He made the disastrous mistake of calling out:

'It's them, Sergeant!'

Hearing his voice, the two reacted instantaneously. Screw hurled the paraffin lamp at the Sergeant, which burst into flame. George jumped to his help and kicked it away before it had time to singe more than the bottom of his trousers. That gave a chance for Chauffeur to run for the far side of the wood and Screw to break away down the path at his top speed – which, as Mike knew only too well, was formidable.

The two detectives set off after him but could not compete. Screw raced for the car and wasted a moment testing the doors without any luck. Then he made a dash for the ruins. The Sergeant and George reached the cloisters not far behind, and were lost to sight except when they appeared at one of the arched openings.

They knew that Screw had not left the ruins but could not tell where he was among all those foundation walls which stood a few feet high. From the ticket window inside the cottage Mike watched George searching the Guest House while Bill kept an eye on the cloisters. Then George covered the cloisters while the Sergeant quickly explored the niches and buttresses of what had been the abbey church.

George passed through an arch and crossed the lawn towards the Library. Screw raised head and shoulders above the low wall.

'Take another step, copper, and it's your last!'

'Put that down and don't be a fool!' George ordered, steadily advancing.

Screw fired. George dropped, clutched his thigh and dragged himself back into the shelter of the cloisters, trailing what looked like a broken leg.

Screw then loosed off two more shots in quick succession, firing uselessly at the cloister wall from which spurts of yellow dust eddied out. The two shots were so close together that any countryman who heard them would think that someone had missed a running rabbit with his first barrel and got it with the second; but to Mike the sharp reports did not sound in the least like those of a shot-gun. He wondered why Screw was wasting ammunition. Perhaps he was testing his pistol to see why he had only broken George's leg instead of killing him?

Sam appeared from the end of the woodland path with his prisoner, trotting the handcuffed Chauffeur in front of him. Chauffeur's coat was torn and he was bleeding at the mouth. Evidently he had not given up without a struggle.

The Sergeant, who was giving first aid to his man, called to Sam to take over. While Sam was applying a dressing to the wound, Chauffeur stood by, desperately talking and talking and making no attempt to run. He was swearing to God that he knew nothing of Screw's gun and that he wasn't responsible. It might be true, Mike thought, for Chauffeur was the least of the three and had not been allowed to see everything.

The Sergeant was too wise to tackle Screw meanwhile, for he had not a hope of reaching him. He had to content himself with a lecture on not surrendering when he was trapped and could never get away. To the horrified Mike it seemed extraordinary that the police were not armed. He knew that they never were in the ordinary daily routine, but thought they would be when out to arrest a bunch of kidnappers. He wished his father or Great-uncle Jim were there. They would have taken cover and blown Screw's head off. He was so angry that he told himself he'd have done it with pleasure if only he had a weapon.

At the same time he was a little ashamed of the thought. That was real blood all over George's legs and the stone beneath them, not the tomato sauce which it was said they used on the telly. It was not right to imagine Screw without a head. Perhaps he had a wife who loved him and anyway it would make one sick. He tried to think of any good reason why Screw should not be killed, but all he could come up with was that the man had made an excellent rabbit stew.

Rabbit stew. There had been an air rifle pellet in it. The rifle might be somewhere in the tents or in their half empty packs.

Unnoticed he slipped out of the front door and putting the cottage between himself and the ruins ran into the wood. He had not far to look. The air rifle was on Screw's bed. A box of pellets was at the bottom of his bag. It appeared an efficient, well-made weapon, but Mike had never used an air rifle. His shooting had all been done under the supervision of his father or Great-uncle Jim with a .22 rifle or a .410 shot-gun. It was no use stalking Screw with a gun he was not sure of.

He found a picture postcard among Screw's belongings and pinned it to a tree with a scarf pin. It took all his strength to load the rifle, which made it certain there would be some power behind the pellet. Then he crossed the clearing and let fly at the postcard. The shot clipped the edge, a little low and left. He reloaded, sighted with more care and was again low and left. Clear enough! There was no wind, so the cause was the rifle. He aimed a trifle high and right and grouped three shots bang in the centre of the postcard. That would do for a sparrow, let alone any selected bit of Screw.

Holding the rifle behind his back he returned to the cottage and settled down behind the low hedge around the garden. He could not see into the cloisters, but he had a good view of Screw who was far out of range. The Sergeant, he thought, was very sensible not to attempt to overpower him even with Sam to help. To get at the gunman from any side it was necessary to cross a stretch of open lawn.

Mike wondered why Screw did not come boldly out of cover, shoot down both policemen and walk off. Possibly he could not make up his mind. The ruins were too much of a maze. If he entered the cloisters through any of the archways, one of them might be able to collar him even if he shot the other.

He saw Screw shift his position so that he could look up the lane. A moment later Mike heard the noise of a motor-cycle. The gardener coming back from mowing the churchyard, of course! From where he was, Mike could not see him. However, the living-room window, under which he had crouched listening to the voices of the kidnappers, was half open. He went through, crossed the room into the kitchen and through its window could follow what was going on.

Screw had crawled quickly round the Library wall and was making a dash for the bike which the gardener had just propped up on its stand. He ordered him to get the hell out, and the gardener got. Keeping lawns neatly mown was one thing; arguing with blokes who pointed a gun quite another.

The Sergeant and Sam saw the danger and ran for the entrance to the lane to cut him off, for there was a chance of knocking him to the ground by a flying tackle before he had gathered speed. He might be able to take a wild shot at one, but the other could grab handlebars or man and bring him down.

Screw, having no doubt about the courage of the police, saw the danger. He dashed back into the cloisters and returned to the car park dragging the wounded George. With his other hand he held the gun to George's head.

'Get back! Right off the car park!' he ordered. 'I've nothing to lose, coppers, if I kill you. Do what you're told or this one gets his now!'

The Sergeant and Sam obeyed. There was nothing they could do, and they were appalled at their wounded companion being dragged along as a helpless hostage.

Very gently Mike opened the window. Screw had to drop George on the ground to get the machine off its stand but he kept the gun pointing down at him. His hand at that angle was a little smaller than the postcard. Mike steadied his elbow on the windowsill. His heart was beating fast and he nearly took an excited snap shot. Then he remembered that his father had told him always to hold his breath when firing a rifle. He did so, sighted a little high and right and squeezed the trigger.

Screw dropped his gun and jumped. The motorcycle fell over and caught his foot. The police, not realising what had happened, started for him a little late. Though Screw was down, he was already reaching for the gun. His outstretched left hand was just lifting it when Mike had reloaded and was ready. There was no time for too careful an aim. He fired low rather than high – the good, sound rule for ground game. This time Screw yelled, and Mike saw blood spurting from his wrist. The pellet had ricochetted off the tarmac and made a long, crippling rip instead of the first puncture which had caused more surprise than damage.

Bill and Sam were on him now, and that was the end. They carried George to a sofa in the cottage – Chauffeur obsequiously offering to help – where Sam continued to dress the wounded leg while the Sergeant kept an eye on his prisoners. They had been so intent on Screw and his hostage that now for the first time they noticed Mike holding the rifle.

'You? You did that?' asked the Sergeant, amazed.

'Well, I saw it all. And I knew he had an air rifle up at their camp.'

'What, that thing! And you aimed at his hand and hit it?'

'It's fairly accurate.'

'You'll get a medal for that, my boy!'

'I don't think I want a medal for shooting people, Sergeant. But it had to be done, hadn't it? Can you keep it quiet?'

'It will have to come out in court, you know, Mike.'

'Oh lord! Will it? And newspapers too? My father won't like that. He always says that if you want to live your own life your own way, keep out of the papers!'

'He does, does he? Well, most people try to get into them.'

'That's because they live in towns and don't feel real.'

'A bit hard on us, aren't you, Mike? Let's have a look at that rifle!'

'It fires a little low and left, Sergeant.'

The Sergeant was tempted to have a shot at a flower

pot on the edge of the car park which he missed by a foot.

'A toy, of course!' he said to cover his embarrassment. 'One has to get used to it. Well, now we can call the Inspector and pick up the last of them. He'll be getting impatient. Twenty minutes we've been at this.'

He spoke over the walkie-talkie.

'Got 'em, sir. But there's been a struggle and Constable Ridgway is shot in the thigh. Leg broken. Ambulance at once, please . . . Yes, Botswinger is still there so far as we know . . . If you drive him up towards us we're armed now . . . Quite, sir. Not unless he fires first . . . No, sir, nothing rash . . . No, sir, I am not at all excited.'

While George remained on guard over Screw and Chauffeur, the Sergeant went out to the lower edge of the ruins where he could watch the hanger. In a few minutes he was back at the cottage.

'They want you down there, Mike.'

'Why? Carrie's all right, isn't she?'

'They hope so. But they can't find her. And Botswinger is not at the spring.'

Mike raced down to the hanger. The Inspector, two of his men and Mr Midwinter were standing by the fox's earth.

'Is this the place you meant, Mike?' he asked.

'Yes. That's where I left her.'

The Inspector put his head and shoulders inside. There was no sign of Carrie.

'All the stuff I stopped the earth with – did you move it?' he asked.

'No, there was nothing in the mouth of the hole. It was all outside, just as it is.'

'Then she must have pushed it all out and left.'

'Or Botswinger found her and pulled it out.'

'Wasn't he watching the spring, sir?'

'No, but he had been there very recently. There's a damp mark of his body still on the stone and two fresh cigarette ends. He is not in the hanger. We have been right through it.'

'And he didn't leave the hanger,' Mr Midwinter added. Not on the two sides I could see, he didn't. And you could see the other sides, Inspector.'

'There's a bit of the top that we couldn't, but if he broke out there he must have run straight up to the Abbey.'

'And then I would have seen him,' Mr Midwinter said.

He strolled off round the hanger to test his opinion. He had the air of being on his own front lawn and standing no nonsense about what anybody could see from where. Evidently he had lost patience with police theories.

'Would you have seen him from the ruins, Mike?' the Inspector asked.

'Not if he went right round them. And the Sergeant and the others were too occupied.'

'If he did, he must have run like hell and got clear before my road block was in position. My chaps report that a car passed them as they were coming up. Only the driver was in it, but Botswinger could have been down on the floor. In that case what warned him? Could he have seen you running for the village?'

'I suppose he could, sir. But if he had seen me he'd have dashed up at once to warn his pals to escape. And he didn't.'

'So it must have been something up at the Abbey which warned him.'

'He would have heard the shots.'

'Three of them, weren't there? Midwinter told us that it was one of his neighbours after pigeons.'

'Two of them were fired at nothing at all,' Mike said.

'Are you sure?'

'Yes, sir. He just fired them at the cloister wall. It could have been a signal.'

'Hmm. Well, we can only hope that Carrie Falconer is not with him.'

There was a yell from Midwinter.

'I've found his gun. Leaning up between two hazel wands it was, with the butt half buried. I wouldn't have seen it in a million years if a little bleeder of a wren hadn't been looking down the barrels for her lunch.'

'Would you please bring it here at once, Mr Midwinter, and very carefully,' the Inspector called.

The police were all silent. Mike looked at the Inspector who looked away. Mr Midwinter came trotting through the bushes and handed over the gun.

'So I was wrong,' he declared cheerfully. 'He got out that way and hid his gun before he ran.'

The Inspector broke open the gun with Mike looking over his arm. They both exclaimed together:

'Thank God!'

Neither of the two cartridges in the breach had been fired.

'The well!' Mike exclaimed. 'We must look in the well at once.'

The whole party left the hanger and hurried up the hill. Two figures were running down to meet them. Mike rushed ahead into the arms of his father and mother.

Tears streamed down his mother's face as she hugged him. His father stroked his head with a very hard and unsteady hand. Mike said that he was all right and that there was nothing wrong with him – only a bit tired.

'And you've got them?' Jack Prowse asked the Inspector.

'Two of them, thanks to this boy of yours. We have missed the third but he won't get far.'

'And Carrie Falconer?'

'We're hoping for the best. She could be with him.'

'She wasn't where I left her when I went for help, Dad,' Mike explained.

'Couldn't you have taken her with you?'

'We had only a minute, you see. They were all round us and meant to kill us if they caught us. And so I hid her and tried to slip through to the police myself.'

'I see. Quite right. You'd have a better chance than she would.'.

'She's become pretty good at it, Dad, but . . . oh, let's go on quick!'

The whole party hurried up to the wood where Mike showed them the hole which led down into the remains of the Abbey barn. Screw and Chauffeur had replaced the brushwood and the ladder. There was no obvious sign of any opening in the bank.

'Wasn't this ever known?' Janet Prowse asked.

'No. The man we want had been warden of the Abbey for a few years,' the Inspector replied. 'He must have found it and kept quiet about it. We have reason to believe he may have used it more than once.'

Mike led the way down.

'Keep round by the wall!' he advised. 'It's not very safe.'

The grating was in place. They lifted it and descended into the arched cellar.

'This is where we were kept.'

The police torches lit up the lines and shadows of arches. Apart from the smell, the only evidence that anyone had been there for the last four hundred years was Mike's home-made poncho.

'And here for days in pitch darkness!' his mother cried in horror.

'Carrie was, and all alone. After they put me down they gave us two candles.'

'They deserve anything they get, those fellows. Everything that's coming to them!' his father growled savagely.

'And the well is through here.'

There were the piled bricks and the open hole. Torches revealed the broken ladder and the black, still water far down which glistened and held its secrets. A handkerchief floated on it.

'She may have been crying when she believed I was dead,' Mike suggested with his voice breaking.

'I've got a rope in my shop,' said Mr Midwinter. 'Back in ten minutes if one of these coppers can drive!'

8

The Fox's Earth

Carrie lay full length well inside the fox's earth. It would have been a comfortable enough resting place after all the desperate activity if it had not been for the pungent, musky smell. At first she was confident that Mike must have got safely away. Down in her burrow she could hear little of what was going on outside – if anything was – but she was sure she would have heard any shot or shouts within the hanger.

The waiting went on and on. She tried to work out how long it would be before rescue – perhaps quarter of an hour for Mike to reach the village and another quarter while he talked to police. It surely could not be more than an hour altogether before she listened to the rumble of approaching voices and a large hand came down to pull her out.

But in loneliness and silence there was no way to tell half an hour from ten minutes. It was a bore to lie there doing nothing, so she wriggled backwards a little further down. Perhaps there would be baby foxes to keep her company. Her left arm went into an opening which might be a rabbit hole or a bit of experimental burrowing by cubs. Her right leg seemed to be kicking around in emptiness; she could bend her leg straight up from the knee without touching anything. She wisely decided that she had gone far enough and it was no time for curiosity and getting buried by a fall. Where she was the soil was firm enough, pressed and polished by the passage of animals, but the rabbit hole was all loose and her right leg had knocked down a shower of earth and pebbles in the course of its explorations.

Wriggling up again towards the mouth, she tried to pass the time looking out through the stoppers which Mike had jammed in the hole and watching a green caterpillar standing on its tail and weaving about, trying to fasten on a twig just out of reach.

At last she heard someone running. The branches were pulled aside. She was just about to call out when feet came down instead of the expected head and shoulders. Before the body filled the hole altogether and cut off the light she had time to see the colour of socks. They were green with a line of black checks up the side. In the gorse she had once been near enough to Beard's feet to recognise them.

He was sweeping the soil outside to cover his footprints, just as Mike had done. Frantically she tried to work out what action to take, wishing she had a syringe and poison for Beard's hairy calves. She thought of biting them hard, but that wouldn't do any good. He might crawl out and then come in head first to deal with her. Did he know she was there? Suppose he had caught Mike and made him confess where she was hidden? But then why had he not come in head first or simply fired a shot down the hole? It began to look very much as if he knew police were on the way and was himself hiding in the one spot he could reach quickly without taking to the open.

Every time he kicked and squirmed she backed further down so that any noise she made was drowned by his own. All that mattered was that he should not discover she was there. He kept sliding down, pushed by knees and elbows, until the soles of his boots were within a foot of her face and her own legs were becoming jammed.

She managed to bend her knees and fit them into the space which her right leg had felt. She twisted her way into it like a snake, and then at last the blind, threatening feet that seemed to hold all Beard's brutality were no longer right on her. She could see nothing. Probably Beard's knees were now across the entrance to her private burrow and his feet had reached the end of the passage.

He lay still for a while, perhaps listening. Having reached the end of the fox's earth, he decided that he need not be so tightly packed and started to heave and kick. It was almost impossible for Carrie to make sense of the commotion. She was certain, however, that one boot had gone through whatever earth and rubble separated her chamber from the main passage. With more room to move the boot searched for something to push against.

She stretched out a nervous hand and found that his boot was up against hard rock, pushing it to drive himself forwards. Suddenly the leg behind the boot shot out straight. She heard a trickle of earth and splashes. Then it seemed that the whole world below her was sliding backwards and she with it. The world above came down in a shower of earth which buried her. There was a roar and a crump. She found herself sitting with the upper part of her free and the rest loosely covered by whatever had collapsed.

She was unhurt beyond bruises and some small cuts on her shoulders from which fingers came away sticky. She was even glad that she was free of those unbearable legs. Darkness was not absolute as it had been after Beard's body filled the hole. Far overhead showed a triangle of light. Mike had never had time to recount all the details of his escape, but he had mentioned the triangle and how thankful he had been to see it. It was unmistakable. Where she had landed must be the underground stream, and she was sure she would be safe there until the police dug down to get her out. Mike could tell them what had happened, and Mike must have got away if Beard was hiding.

She extricated herself and slid down a slope of rubble without bothering how much noise she made. Immediately the beam of a torch picked her up. Reflection from the limestone allowed her to make out the bulk of a human being with a dark beard. She screamed in terror and was answered by a roar:

'So we're back together again!'

She plunged and plodded down the rest of the slope, coming out on to hard rock at the bottom. She raced down the channel of the stream, trying to remember all that Mike had told her about it and realising – in a sort of dream picture rather than any thought – that the dip in the ground which held the fox's earth must be above the landfall over which Mike had climbed. Beard was close behind her but limping badly. She knew that from the splashing. Instead of a regular splash-splash of fast feet, they went splash-pause-splosh-splash. If only she could keep ahead of this wounded beast she must come to the pool of which Mike had told her.

The beam of the torch behind her wavered, sometimes holding her so that she could not escape into any side passage if there was one, sometimes lighting the channel for Beard. That was useful because it prevented her tripping over stones which were agony to her bare feet. She dared not look back to see how close he was. Once he seemed within grabbing distance; once he yowled with pain and there was a second or two before the splosh-splash restarted.

She saw faint, diffused light ahead of her and then the pool. It was very different from the picture she had made for herself after Mike's brief description. It was not at all beautiful. It was a dark, dead end. At the brink the water was indeed calm and greenish, but farther out it swirled beneath ledges and between rocks, all smooth and rounded by aeons of floods. The roof was very low and the outlet to the spring not at all obvious.

She waded in, hoping that Beard could not swim. He did not have to. He ripped off coat and trousers and waded in after her up to his chest. She could not find the round boulder which Mike said he had shifted. She had never seen it from the outside and could not distinguish it from the rock face. She wasted time diving in a panicky effort to get through a lit opening which was barely big enough for a fish. When she had to come up for air, Beard was within yards of her. The main current was gently swirling against his waist, and he was blocking what must be the correct way out.

'Come on, sweetie!' he ordered, holding out his arms.

The roof came down so close to the water that he could not reach her without stooping and putting his head under. He hesitated. Carrie guessed that he did not want to get head, shirt and shoulders wet. If they were, he would be suspect to everyone who saw him after his escape.

She dived again, feeling her way like a crab under a smooth ledge of rock from which she hoped it might be difficult to haul her out. But the recess did not go back far enough. She took two more kicks with lungs bursting and cautiously broke the surface without a ripple. Where she had come up it was black night – a miniature bay cut off from the seeping daylight of the spring. The beam of the torch was searching for her. She had time to hide her head behind a jagged rock fallen from the roof, the tip of which was just above water.

Beard had retreated a little from his position and was flashing his torch along the surface of the pool. She was sure she had puzzled him. He was only visible as a dark bulk in a green shadow, but he was turning and peering in all directions. It was possible that he now thought he had blocked the wrong place and that she had found the way out. There was an eddy which had helped to carry her under the recess, and he would have felt it against his legs. She dared not move or hope until she saw him wade out and put on coat and trousers. Then he limped splash-pause-splosh up the channel again. She asked herself what Mike would do now. The answer was clear. Make sure that he has really given up and then take your time!

Creeping along behind him in the darkness, she saw him begin to climb the sloping slab of rock half covered with debris. That was good enough. He was getting out. The landslip must have left a considerable crack on the surface within easy reach. And if the police had not yet arrived at the hanger he was the sort of criminal to have a plan for escape worked out long beforehand.

She returned down the channel – her feet more sore than ever with no torch to guide them and no terror to take her mind off them – and plunged into the water again. She had no more doubt where the outlet was, for Beard had shown her. Her first two attempts failed. That boulder which blocked the way was never going to move even an inch from where it had settled after Mike and the current had jammed it; but there was just room for a child who was very determined and accustomed to swim under water. Carrie was both, and on her third attempt she was through into the sunlight of the pool. She had half expected somebody to be there to receive her, but there was no one – no Mike, no Rupert and Mary, no police. The hanger was quite silent except for the cooing of a dove.

She could not make up her mind what to do. It seemed wise not to run for the Abbey and to stay in cover in case Screw and Chauffeur were still about. She crept up as far as the fox's earth. The mouth of it was just as it always had been. All around it the earth was pitted with footmarks as if an army had walked over. Among them she spotted the smaller prints of Mike and sat down sobbing with relief.

So he and the police had been there and she was free

at last wherever the criminals were. But before she ran out of the hanger she looked to see whether the collapse had left an opening through which Beard could have escaped. She found it in a thicket of elder beyond the dip in which was the earth and outside the range of the footmarks. There the ground had slipped down in a rough circle and the upper end of the slide was crossed by a crack easily wide enough to allow Beard's body to pass.

Everybody must now be at the Abbey. All the same she approached it cautiously, first taking cover behind the long, dry-stone wall. Then on the skyline she saw the top of a uniformed policeman and heard in the distance the wailing of an ambulance siren. She limped painfully up the hill on to the blessedly soft lawns among the ruins. The car park was full of cars. It swarmed with press photographers and men with notebooks.

She shivered in the wind, standing in nearly the same corner of the Library where Screw had drawn his gun. Nobody noticed her. People scuttled about without any single object like disturbed ants round their nest. Some were apparently demanding to be let into the cottage and being held back by a policeman. A tall Inspector had a knot of men and women round him all talking at once. A truck with a TV camera had come down the lane and stopped. She was ashamed of her appearance and afraid of so many strangers. There was nobody she knew to comfort her.

And then it was that Mike came through an opening in the cloisters, walking between a plump, very pretty woman and a tall, dark man so like him that he had to be his father.

'Carrie!' he shouted and ran to her.

She was dripping water and her rags were stained with the mud and earth of days which even the spring pool could not wash away. Her hair stuck to her face in rat tails; but that face was all Mike looked at. There was nothing to set it off or conceal its shape. He had never noticed before how fine-drawn and gallant it was.

He hugged her, asking again and again what had happened.

'I came out of the spring like you did, Mike.'

'He threw you down the well?'

'No. He hid on top of me in the fox's earth and it all collapsed. And then he gave up chasing me and got away.'

'My poor darling!' Janet Prowse exclaimed, gathering her up. 'Jack, run and get the car rug! Mike, fetch her parents out from all those news hounds!'

Mike approached the ring of excited, bobbing heads. Rupert and Mary had arrived only five minutes earlier. The photographers around the Prowses had immediately dispersed to take pictures of the film star. That had given the family time to slip away to the cloisters and longed-for privacy.

He thought that the Falconers, too, and especially Carrie, would like to be reunited without people looking on who had no business to look. So he found the Sergeant and whispered to him that Carrie was safe and in the ruins. Could he get Mr and Mrs Falconer a moment's peace?

The Sergeant half let out a whoop of relief and turned it into a cough. He extracted Rupert and Mary, led them towards the ruins and there told them the good news. But Mike's efforts were all in vain.

'Carrie! Carrie is safe!' the actor shouted, turning round to his audience.

Carrie ran to her parents, dropping on the way the car rug in which she was wrapped. Rupert and Mary knelt on the grass beside her, and all three were alone for a moment to show their love and joy. Then Rupert picked her up and posed for the cameras. Mary had to do the same and they all had to kiss each other over again.

A TV man pushed a microphone at Carrie.

'Tell us all about your escape! Don't be shy! Come on, sweetie!'

'Get out! Get out, all of you!' she screamed. 'Rupert, tell them to go away!'

The Sergeant rescued her and put back the rug, saying:

'We need her statement at once, gentlemen, and want her to be in a state to give it.'

'Of course she can give it,' Mike told him. 'It's only that Beard used to call her sweetie.'

Mr Midwinter was back with his coil of rope. He had a word with the driver of the police car and again screamed off in the direction of his village. The speed, the rope and his sudden disappearance fascinated a reporter who shot off after him in the hope of a story which none of his competitors would have.

The Inspector led the Prowses and Falconers into the cottage and shut the door. Screw and Chauffeur had been driven off with blankets over their heads. The living-room was empty. Somebody had thrown a table-cloth over the bloodstains. Carrie and Mike were given chairs opposite the Inspector.

'Couldn't you wait?' Mary Falconer asked. 'The child is exhausted. She needs a hot bath and a hot drink.'

'I'm afraid we cannot wait, madam.'

'Well, you'll bloody well have to!' replied Janet Prowse, and the two mothers carted Carrie off before the startled Inspector had time to protest.

Meanwhile Mike told his story and answered questions as best he could.

'You must be very proud of him indeed,' the Inspector said to Jack Prowse.

'Well, all in the day's work! And would you believe it? A chap out there has just offered me five thousand quid for his exclusive story.'

'I shouldn't let that bother you. You take it! He'll write it himself or one of his pals will.'

'A pack of lies, I suppose?'

'Most of it. So what do you care?'

'I hadn't looked at it that way,' said Jack Prowse. 'Then as long as we can have a good laugh, there's no harm done. What do you think, Mike?'

'We could buy that ten acres of scrub and put 'em down to grass.'

'But it's your money.'

'Well, we'll always be partners, Dad, won't we?'

'I've always hoped so, son.'

'You should use it to give him a good education,' Rupert Falconer said.

'Anything wrong with what he's had, Mr Falconer?'

The invaluable Mr Midwinter put his head round the door.

'Clothes for her,' he announced. 'Been through the

wife's stock again! Best I could do in a hurry. A pity she's out.'

He laid on a chair a boy's jeans, shirt and two sweaters, coolly asked Rupert Falconer for his autograph and remarked that he would be outside if he was wanted.

The clothes were sent upstairs and soon afterwards the two women brought down Carrie, looking like a pale but composed young boy instead of the pitiable drowned kitten who had been hurried away. The Inspector had already heard the main facts of her story from Mike and now quickly concentrated on the end of it.

'So the last you saw of Botswinger – Beard, as you call him – was climbing up the fall to get out. We'll go and see how he did it. And you keep them all off till we've finished, Bill! I don't want that ground trampled worse than it is. Carrie, do you feel up to it?'

Carrie answered cheerfully that she did, but that she hadn't any shoes.

'Oh, I've got those,' the Inspector said. 'We picked them up by the spring where you told Mike to leave them. And that was a bright idea if there ever was one, young woman! It saved the pair of you.'

Down again in the hanger, she showed them where the surface had slipped. The police had only been interested in the fox's earth, and anyone standing by the mouth would have noticed nothing out of the ordinary beyond it – even Mike had not, though now he spotted the change.

'Those two elders have got all tangled up with each other,' he said. 'They must be leaning.'

They were. So were most of the others, growing thickly over rank ground disturbed by generations of foxes and badgers. The surface had sunk not quite in a circle as Carrie had described it, but in an oval along the course of the underground stream. Where the slide had started, it had opened a chasm easily wide enough for Beard's escape. When the Inspector shone a torch down it the beam showed an irregular pile of earth and stones up which a man could have crawled with ample room for his head. The flow of water beneath it could be heard.

He left a constable on guard to see that nothing was disturbed, and the rest of them began to return up the hill. Meanwhile Jack Prowse was pacing out distances with all the gravity of a farmer.

'Do you mind if I just run over the ground with my son?' he asked. 'I want to see how on earth he managed to lie low when they were beating out the hanger.'

'Certainly, Mr Prowse,' the Inspector agreed.

'Oh, come on, Jack!' Janet said. 'Mike doesn't want to go through all that again.'

But Mike was already pointing out the ivy where he had taken refuge and the strip of bramble which had hidden Carrie.

'And now show me the spring!' his father asked.

Mr Prowse was so interested in it that he waded in and tried the round boulder by the side of which Mike and Carrie had managed to squeeze out.

'Well, nothing but a crowbar is ever going to move that again,' he said. 'Tell me all about that awful journey of yours out of the well and down the channel!'

They sat on the bank above the fox's earth. Jack held

his hand while Mike tried to recapture far more details than he had had time to explain to his father or the police and told how the way had been blocked and how he had climbed over and down the sloping, fallen rock to regain the stream.

'Did you ever look in the hanger for that opening which gave you a little light? The triangle?'

'Not a chance, Dad! Too busy.'

'Well, we have time now. Let's see!'

They quickly found it, not far from the bank and between two moss-covered rocks.

'Dangerous, that!' Jack Prowse remarked. 'When the hunt comes through here, a horse could easily break its leg in this hole.'

He found a fallen hazel with the mat of earth still attached to its roots, dragged it out and shoved it down the hole. Then he went to look at the crack by which Beard might have escaped.

'Where most of that new lot slid down must have been a bit upstream from the earlier fall,' he said.

'Yes, Dad.'

'Well, we can leave it to the police to catch him. You're my only son, Mike, and I shall never feel sorry, not for a moment, if this Botswinger chap gets all he deserves.'

They returned to the Abbey. The crowd had thinned. The TV camera had gone, and so had the Falconers. Mr Midwinter was still there. He said that the police were exploring the cellars and had gone down the well. He was waiting to see that he got his rope back.

'You'll want your boy's clothes back, too,' Janet Prowse said.

'Any time that's convenient. Parcel post. The wife will be glad to have them.'

'Where is he? At school?'

'Captain in the Army, Mrs Prowse. Time passes. No getting away from it. I never did like that Botswinger. But he was a neighbour and so we only spoke ill of him among ourselves, if you see what I mean, though a funny lot of men they were who used to drive up to see him from time to time. They're the chaps who will know where he is, and I've told the Inspector so.'

Mike was bitterly disappointed that her parents had dragged Carrie away to hospital, alarmed by her bruises and the state of her feet; but he saw plenty of her in the months to come when they met in the law courts and had to tell their stories over and over again. Maximum sentences were handed out to Screw and Chauffeur. Beard himself remained at large, though the police were sure they knew the route by which he had escaped from England, and Interpol kept watch on the ring of international crooks for whom they believed he had worked. The only other person in trouble was Rupert Falconer who had no right at all to have a Swiss bank account. It took him three more successful films before he could settle the fine he got for not paying his taxes as well as the taxes themselves.

The Prowses and the Falconers drifted apart, having nothing much in common; but Mike and Carrie never lost touch and were free at last to see as much as they liked of each other when Mike was studying estate management and Carrie in her first year at university.

They never talked much about those terrible days six years earlier. They had had quite enough of that in the witness box and among their friends. But at a dance in Mike's college Carrie spoke of it all again when after supper they were walking in the garden before the disco started up once more.

'I wonder what did happen to Beard,' she said.

'I wondered too – for a long time.'

'You know, Mike?'

'I think I know and I think my father did. After we were left alone in the hanger he tested that boulder in the stream and he asked me a whole lot of questions. I couldn't see the point of them at the time.'

'What were they about?'

'Oh, he was working out the distance between the old landfall and the new one which carried you and Beard down with it. You remember the dome with the triangle of light in it and the sloping rock?'

'I'll never forget them.'

'Just before I got there, the roof of the channel was only a little above my head and very shaky. That was what fell down, and you were lucky that most of it was behind you.'

'So was Beard!'

'And it was straight downstream that he chased you.'

Carrie shivered.

'The beast! Mike, I came alive again when he turned back and I saw him climbing out!'

'But you didn't hang around to see if he got out. And I don't blame you!'

'Well, he could easily have reached that big crack. The police were quite sure.'

'Yes, he could easily have done it if he had been upstream on the Abbey side of the fall. But he wasn't, Carrie darling.'